Halflife

ISBN:0-9820630-0-8
ISBN-13:978-0982063002
Library of Congress Control Number: 2008936049

To order additional copies of this book,
visit www.amazon.com or www.InnerformsLtd.com

First InnerformsLtd.com Paperback Edition

Halflife

Anthony Alofsin

Innerforms Ltd

For my sister, Margot Alofsin
(1952–2008)

Because nothing is as surprising as life.
Except for writing. Except for writing.
Yes, of course, except for writing, the only consolation.

— Pamuk, *The Black Book*

HALFLIFE

No one in the family has lived past the age of seventy. I doubt I will be the exception, so now that I have reached the year that approximates half my life, I will mark the event by observing the world around and within me with some observations about animals, plants, people, and other matters in a series of random notes that I call Halflife. Their motifs reflect a recurrent theme, the decay of matter. Matter has its own limited existence. In scientific terms half-life is a great measuring stick, providing the time period in which a radioactive isotope loses half its atoms. Of the some 1650 species of atoms known as isotopes, only 335 occur in nature. In that natural group about sixty-five are radioactive, but we have created over a thousand artificial examples. Carbon-14 ,discovered in 1940, has a half-life of 5,730 years. Its number comes from the fourteen protons and neutrons in its nucleus. When atoms decay, they give off particles called alpha, beta-plus, or beta minus, and these emitted particles create daughter atoms. This is the primordial process of decay and change and creation. Every thing, every person is disordered, disintegrating, rotting, falling apart, encumbering dust, dirt, mold, fungus, and bodily illness.

MOUNTAINS

Smoke still swirled from the charred wood posts. In the most primitive houses built in rural New Mexico wood imbedded with mud passed for walls, but while the mud will not burn, the wood can ignite under intense heat and burn from within. Such an intense heat had leveled the two-room, L-shaped house in the country near a village where the Pecos River valley opens for the first time as the river descends south from the Sangre de Cristo mountains. I had stored my possessions, including my sculpture and books, in the attic of the small house. The weavings were still in San Francisco. One morning a friend called to say the house had caught fire. No fire departments existed for such places in the country nor was there much water of any sort. Acting as if there was no point in telling me earlier, the friend called two days after the fire had started. By the time I drove out to the country I found only piles of ash, fragments of pages from some of my books, and a twisted pair of psychedelic granny glasses. The fire had incinerated all the sculptures. The mud of the adobe chinking had spalled off to leave only the charred timbers. In the following spring a neighbor planted corn where the walls had been. When the rains came, the seeds began to grow so that the old mud walls became lines of green stalks.

The place of the fire hugged the bottom of an escarpment that formed the side of a mesa in the middle of the river valley. From the top of the mesa, the view west extended beyond the little black smudge over irrigated fields and the curling Pecos River to the towering sides of Rowe Mesa. To the east lay a flanking mesa marking the beginning of the high staked planes and the limits of primordial erosion. The valley closed to the south, but to the north the view opened to the mountains behind Santa Fe, covered in pines and even snow into the early summer months.

In my last year of college in the early 1970s what I knew about New Mexico was only that it was far away and exotic. Long before its discovery by the chic and wealthy, Santa Fe was still a village that sheltered its locals and charmed its new residents. A sleepy place with three steamy bars, it was also where an old Japanese artist, having finished his life work, could be seen looking straight into the sun, blinding himself, and smiling. The fabled light, the sky, the unapproachable Indians of the pueblos, moved me.

Having refused to enter the family business, I went to Santa Fe to sculpt. Disapproving of such an insecure life style and hurt by my refusal, my father cut me off financially and withdrew all other support. I enjoyed the odd jobs that supported a modest life style, but then my father grew ill and died of a brain tumor in his fifty-fourth year. Mother had died five years earlier, so at the age of twenty-two I became an adult orphan. Santa Fe became a place of grieving.

One day while heading to water the snow peas at the small farm I shared with my good friend, Eddie, I stepped on a thorny seed—a goat's head—on the flagstone floor of the portale. The goat's head, *Tribulus terrestris*, a member of the Caltrop family, is a plant with yellow flowers five to ten millimeters across and spiny fruits, which are called by the name of the plant. The fruit separates into five bony carpals, and those prickly bodies can measure up to seven millimeters in length. A goat's head is about as thick as three pennies stacked on top of each other. A rough ridge divides the goat's head into two symmetrical parts. The head slopes down from the ridge on each side to terminate at its upper part into two round, sharp thorns. The back of the head is roughly textured and shows the break between the head and the plant part that grew it.

The goat's head has only two purposes: to transport the seed within it and to bedevil the feet of people and animals. For a small thorn its spiny horns cause a serious pain. They hurt the feet of children who go barefoot, and dogs can be seen licking them from the pads of their paws. Goat's heads have been known to kill livestock who foolishly ate them. As an organic bit of matter the goat's head decays much more slowly than a cottonwood leaf. Its hardness keeps it actively inflicting pain long after many softer thorns have turned to dust.

The name comes from the resemblance between the thorn and the head of a goat in miniature. Having extracted the goat's head, I held it between my fingers and could see it also resembled the head of a medieval demon, something similar to the devil in Dürer's engraving, *The Knight, Death, and Devil*, except that the horns of the sticker were straight. The goat's head thorn also resembled the face of a vampire bat, or the wizened, shrunken head of a buffalo.

Cleared of the thorn, I drove to town for the last night of my job as a waiter at the Pink Adobe, a quaint restaurant with aspirations beyond the mundane. The next day I would start new work as an assistant in an architect's office where the big project was the documentation of Socorro, a poor place in central New Mexico whose best days as a Wild West boom town declined with the demonetization of silver in 1873. Fortunately, a local photographer had extensively documented the town with images made on large glass plate negatives. His photographs showed that the town had been beautiful in its simplicity and imbued with devotion: annually he documented the lines of people crawling to church for blessings on the feast of Corpus Christi. Some views the photographer shot at eye level, others from a roof of one of the mercantile stores, so the full cortege could be seen winding through the town and the mountains to the west where its smelters had been.

Socorro's poverty had protected it: no economic incentive could be found in tearing down its nineteenth century architecture, so much of it, though crumbling, was intact. In the course of documenting its houses and buildings, I met Billy Giddings, a man who not only knew the town's history but also collected its artifacts, assembling a hoard that contained objects of historical value for the whole Southwest. Proud of his collection, Billy turned part of his house into a museum. He had obtained much of his artefacts from local attics, but he also had secret sources. His specialties were objects of gold and pre-civil war newspapers. In Socorro, where he was born and lived all his life, his father had been one of the first Anglo settlers after the silver boom. A handsome man, the father was a lawyer, but also an alcoholic, who died when Billy was a baby. For his whole life Billy cared for his mother in the house he still occupied. Billy, his wife, who was fifteen when they married, and his mother lived together happily until the mother's death.

The people of the town did not appreciate Billy's museum. They did not grasp the historic value of the diary of the first white missionary to visit the territory, nor did they find any excitement in a newspaper dated 1860, or the ancient Indian pots that Billy had procured from nearby ruins. Few people came to see the museum, and when it closed, a bitterness began simmering within him.

Billy next opened a nightclub with a spacious dance floor on the east end of town. In some ways Club Owner seemed like Billy's ideal profession. The darkness of bars, talk of women and adventure, and card playing were natural to him, with one exception: Billy did not get along with people in general. He was a loner at heart. By the time I met him in his early seventies he had only a few friends, and the best of those were his wife and two dogs.

The nightclub operated only a few months before the state seized his land for the new highway that would skirt the eastern edge of town. He fought the seizure because he felt the state was not paying him for his investment in the club. He lost his case, which made him more resentful than ever. From that time onward Billy despised federal, state, and local government, as well as any museum, which he saw as just another political institution.

He was strong the first time we met, his memory clear, his wit sharp. There was something of the fox about Billy, a cunning quality that had assisted him in making a living. It was never clear how he had made money; some people guessed gambling. It is certain that he and his wife owned rental properties, and some said he had an inheritance from his mother.

Billy spoke slowly to me. He avoided answering questions directly and often slipped into a reverie that had nothing to do with our conversation. He knew the value of the Spanish-era treasures that he had sequestered in his vault, and whenever he described them, he would watch me out of the corner of his eye to see if I coveted them.

• • •

Sometimes driving on my way south to Socorro I would wander off the main highway and explore random landscapes, the Indian ruins at Quarai, and once, the *Jornado del Muerto*. Often mistranslated as the Journey of the Dead, the phrase referred to the Journey of the Dead Man to mark a blistering, flat desert that decimated early Spanish settlers who were heading

north in search of the Seven Cities of Cibola. On cross-
ing this desiccated land in 1598, the travelers gave the
first pueblo they found the name of Nuestra Senora del
Socorro for the hope it offered them; the town retained
the abbreviated name. Bitterly arid and desolate, the
plains of the *Jornado* later provided the testing site for
the Alamogordo Bombing and Gunnery Range where
the government detonated the first atomic bomb in July
1945. Conceived at Los Alamos, 230 miles to the north,
the bomb proved that atomic fission could create the ul-
timate weapon and means of human annihilation. With
fission came not only destruction, but awareness of the
death of matter. Particles now danced rhythms known
only previously to the sun.

• • •

In those days before AIDS random encounters re-
sulted in amorous adventures, some brief in duration,
others longer. Santa Fe was full of strange people. My
encounters usually occurred at the end of winter, and
soon had a pattern: passion erupted, brief joy followed,
and the long separation began. Within this cycle, a hope
of permanence lurked in response to some unconscious
effort to counter all-pervasive decay. My love life was a
weak human way of preventing the escape of particles
from primordial isotopes.

Marli was one of those encounters. She had grown
up at the remote edge of town on flat land that dipped
on the west toward a series of springs that flowed into
the Santa Fe river. Her house was modest, and the plot
around it, barren. Her family had come from rural stock

who had long ago intermarried with Indians as they moved west from Tennessee and Oklahoma. They had been poor dirt farmers who now had jobs in construction or worked for the railroad.

Marli grew up in isolation from the ways of the town but in the company of books, and, in particular, the presence of her father, lately deceased. He had worked on the railroad, a job that took him often away from home. According to the daughter, his true calling was that of an inventor. When he was home, he spent his time on a special invention: a telescope. For the telescope he used the finest optically ground lenses he could obtain. The stars had a fascination for him that he passed to the daughter. From childhood onward she spent much time projecting herself into other nebula and alien realms.

Marli's body was a perfect landscape of natural proportion: the length between her hips was a meadow flanked at its sides by smooth escarpments. Her breasts were like the hills to the south swelling up smooth and symmetrical. She had the smoothest skin I had ever felt; its whiteness came from her Anglo-Saxon blood. Strong bones defined her face. Her nose was straight and sharp, a sign of her Cherokee and Apache blood, inherited through her mother's side. Her eyes were large and blue, and always widely open. Yet her face showed a subtle erosion, with fine lines around her eyes and mouth that resembled the delicate cuts in the sandstone of dry arroyos.

We came from different worlds, and perhaps that difference itself created an attraction of inverse being. Some part of me responded to her disconnection from ordinary life. After two minutes of listening to her extraterrestrial accounts, anyone would say that she was strange. Beautiful and tall, she also appeared too fragile to survive. If her father was meant to be an inventor, Marli's true calling was less clear. She had spent her working life in clerical jobs at the government agencies that supplied the main source of the town's employment. In these jobs she performed trivial functions, so that few people realized they were in the presence of a highly unusual person who spent much time imagining she was on other planets. If you listened closely, instead of dismissing her simply as strange, you would see that she had an extraordinary way of using words. This may have been the result of her particular knowledge, spawned by thoughts of other galaxies, or from communications with their inhabitants, or through other various studies. In one sentence she would focus on the mundane – *The baby already has learned to look through a camera*—in the next she would plunge to the core—*You look different than I remember, you are heavier, it's not your weight, its the burden you have been carrying.* The effect was that of a stranger describing your condition with total, concise accuracy.

I found this duality of speech unsettling, particularly when she spoke about the suffering she had experienced. Listening to her made me feel caught between ordinary life and the ether. Her pain had come from poverty, from the frustration of being a clerk when she wanted to study and know the stars. Her pain came from her father's death, a deep loss for her and her mother.

There were moments, however, when her suspension between real and imagined worlds ceased. That cessation occurred when we explored each other's hands, when our bodies rolled together, revolution after revolution the whole length of a room, or when the flat parts of our tongues touched. Some male and female connectors plugged together at those moments, and grounded us to the earth. Orgasm meant little in the hold of our connection. I never satisfied her as other men did. *Why don't you use your fingers?* she asked me.

When we first met, she was single, but later she had a child who brought her more pain. A handsome young Texan had fathered the sickly child, but he left Marli for a rich woman in Dallas. After the child was born, the soft skin of Marli's face lost all its color except for a tinge of blue from the subsurface veins. Her eyes grew glassy, sunken, and hollow. A rapid ageing had started that afflicts the poor.

I saw her only occasionally, but always noticed how she aged too quickly. Eventually, she disappeared. Or was I the one who disappeared?

• • •

I met Anna in Santa Fe through a mutual friend who introduced us over lunch held underneath the shade of an umbrella. A summer dress hung on her loosely as if the wind had tossed a translucent silk sheet around her bare skin. She wore black glasses that hid her eyes. A wide-brimmed hat protected her face from the sun. Her three-year old daughter was at her side.

No lines marked her Anna's face, no speck of pigment dotted the continuous tone of her skin. Only one error showed: lips that had once been so perfect they appeared in an advertisement on television, were no longer perfect. An incautious driver had pulled out of his lane in a narrow canyon north of the city and smashed her jeep. Anna went through the window, crushing her top lip. Plastic surgery had fixed its ragged edges so that only an eye at close distance could notice that her lips were not exactly symmetrical, that the smooth texture of the top lip had been abraded.

Anna and I made plans to meet late in the afternoon when the child was asleep. Our meeting took place south of town on a road that crossed the dry, grassy mesas on flat land in that part of the county. The road to our meeting place curved slowly, rising to a view of the Jemez mountains to the west and the Sangre de Christo mountains to the east. I had suggested meeting there because we could see both mountain ranges at once.

She was free of her responsibilities for a few moments, from her child, and her recent divorce. Released, standing on ancient soil, gazing at igneous mountains whose eroded surface had made the earth beneath us, we smiled and stared into each other until the colored clouds of sunset marked the time for her return. We drove back to town and planned to meet again.

• • •

I traveled often in the countryside to visit the small villages of northern New Mexico. Sometimes I saw friends in the Pecos River valley where the great flat mesas opened up to give the river breathing space and allowed the planting of rich irrigated fields. During one of those sojourns my friends gave me a young dog. We discerned that she came from a lineage of local dogs, whose origins were traced to a dog called Mule (who had a twin, Egg) then to Moe, sired by Mule, who mated with a wild coyote. Many of the canines in the region mated between species, mixing collie, German shepherd, coyote, and assorted mongrels, but they told no one of their secret lives or their family roots.

I named my dog Minerva, but we all called her Minnie. An extraordinary creature, she had an unusual sensitivity to all things around her. Staring at me with her chestnut eyes, she spoke with every glance. Sometimes the sadness of her eyes reminded me of my grandfather. Although frightened by loud noises, such as car horns, and terrified by thunder and the sound of gun shots, she could be fierce. When we camped out in mountain country, she would paw the ground to make a little bed for herself in the dirt, twenty to thirty feet from where I slept, and watch over me all night long. No coyotes or other night creatures could approach without her sounding a fierce alarm. Also, she could run fast and keep up with Mariah, the big thoroughbred I rode in those days. Occasionally I would put Minnie in match races with other dogs; she always won.

Not only did Minnie have a deep spirit that made her far more interesting than most humans, but she had a nurturing way. After I showered, she would lick my legs to dry them. And if ever I had a lover stay over and shower, she would lick her legs too. People always asked after her, their thoughts focused on her pure love.

• • •

Anna and I met again. Some sense of shared reality that I had experienced with her returned, but there was a strangeness in the connection between us and our mutual attraction. She moved with grace and smiled. Her radiant face expressed openness. Relaxed, she spoke directly and simply, but I worked feelings through thought. She appeared open in ways I was closed. I felt, nevertheless, as if I were seeing into this powerful woman, not by choice, and perceiving her most private self. I do not know what she saw within me, but I remember thinking *You have stirred me. I enjoy the trembling and dance in the fear.*

• • •

The mornings in Santa Fe were reveries in dry light. On a rare occasion, however, the air of the mountain town filled with moisture. When slow moving, amorphous clouds greeted the day, and the air smelled of the sea, I wondered if a cataclysm had occurred west of the Jemez mountains and the Pacific ocean lapped at the land's edge. Perhaps the ancient sea, once here for millions of years, had re-emerged to round river stones, calling out for their watery ancestors. On the east side of the mountains, little fingers of land, once tiny islands surrounded by sea life, presently floated in the air. The smallest islands imaginable, they were now covered with piñon trees and streaked with high security fences behind which nuclear weapons were perfected. The creatures and plants of the ancient sea were everywhere. Carbon dating revealed their ages. On the road called Cerro Gordo (Fat Hill), fossils lay scattered for the taking. Sea shells, hidden in dull looking rocks, yielded to the tap of a hammer. Further to the south of town, a hiker could find trilobites, great conoidal mollusks, in a place called Waldo that was no place, only a sign on the highway. At both Cerro Gordo and Waldo lay fossils of a most ancient species of vegetative life, an ancestor of bamboo that consists of flat cylinders piled on top of each other. Liquid minerals had replaced their innards eons ago. The skeletons of fish were more rare, but they appeared after the rains.

So this land, thought of as desert, was an ancient ocean itself at the whim of grey clouds. When the clouds moistened the air, the land became more watery than the great living oceans. This place, full of memory, exuded the ancient sea in the self.

• • •

I was living in a compound of old adobe buildings in town. In the morning sun I often sat and waited for hummingbirds to come to the feeder. Once, suddenly in the grassy courtyard between the potting shed and the house, a starling began shrieking. So incessant and shrill was its call that Minnie sat up and turned her head. At the call of the shrieker, fifteen starlings gathered in the misshapen willow in the courtyard. All oriented in the same direction, they began warning everyone about the gray cat, the fiercest hunter in the compound, who was leering in his hiding place below a bird's nest under the eaves. The birds had come together to face the attacker. The gray cat growled a long, low vibration that communicated a vicious strength to kill. What surprised me was not the cat's sound, but the starlings' shriek that brought together a flock. Their reunion in formation against the cat lasted only a minute, but it was an impressive warning and act of resistance. Just as suddenly as they had assembled, they flew away. Until that time, I had always seen starlings as dull birds with unpretty voices and aggressive ways that kept other beautiful solitary birds away from the garden, but my respect for the small black shriekers suddenly grew.

• • •

Anna and I met again at my room in the compound where we pulled each other into a bed covered in loose sheets. My lips touched the nipples of her breasts, and she moaned a sound I was to hear often, a sound not wholly human, yet low and rolling like the chant of Tibetan monks. But she pulled away suddenly: her daughter needed tending; she got up, and drove away in the dark. Two days later we lay together again. My hands went right through her body. She said she could feel I was a little afraid, but she said that must be how people walk through walls. What was it I said, after making love, something about shaking a star inside her until it glowed, and I felt the tributaries flowing from the Himalayas?

We unfolded our experiences to each other, recounting the little events that make up memory. She did say her ex-husband abused women, that he had beaten her up, and that he had sudden violent surges. She said nothing about her child, but the next time I saw her three-year old daughter I noticed a long, red scar under her chin. The ex-husband had thrown her onto the floor in a rage and caused the laceration.

• • •

In those days I drove around town in a turquoise, 1952 Ford pick up truck. I bought Merlin, as I called him, from a fellow in Sacramento who kept the truck very cherry and had purchased it directly from the Sierra Nevada fire department. Consequently, Merlin had fewer owners than most people have spouses. Built with three on a column when synchromesh was a pipe dream, the truck had double compound low gears. The engine was also the first model to have the valves on its top, not on the side. Merlin liked long straight roads without much incline. Gliding along, you were a king of the road, the envy of every eye. Truckers knew you were driving a class vehicle, and anybody with a feel for old trucks appreciated the beauty of the machine. The ride was smooth on those long stretches, but the truck was a chore to drive in the city. No power brakes, no power steering, so Merlin needed strong arms and legs. The suspension was so rigid that your vertebrae shook if you drove over pot holes. Instead of coils, Merlin had flat leaf springs, blades of steel wrapped together above each wheel. Also, curves were not much fun as the low center of gravity made going around corners a risk to roll-over. Anna scared herself nearly to death the first time she tried to drive Merlin. We went around a corner a bit too fast, and she thought all was lost. She never wanted to drive Merlin again. Too bad, but maybe Merlin did not like women driving him.

• • •

The weight of memory pulled me to the earth in a land of the sky, to the earth and under it as I wondered where was Billy's grave. He often returned to my thoughts in the morning as I surveyed the vista from the compound portale. I recalled him as an old man in his pajamas and robe. He had a pearl-handled derringer in his robe pocket. His wife was driving us to a park in early evening, which was a significant outing for the nearly bedridden Billy. The light was fading, and Billy took the derringer into his hand so no one would mess with him in his helpless state. The heat poured out of everything the sun had touched. We watched the dogs running in the park, and Billy told stories of how his father came to the boom town as a young lawyer in the 1880s, of the gold Billy had in his safe, and the diary of an early explorer he had hidden in a box in the ground. We returned to Billy's house and ate red chili and white bread.

I heard from neighbors that Billy died shortly after that visit. I have never seen his grave. The last time I went to pay my respects to his widow, she remembered me only as some person from the vague past, a visitor with "big bulging eyes."

• • •

One day Anna and I stood at the edge of Valle Grande, the great volcanic caldera in the Jemez Mountains, and although it was mid-winter, the sun warmed us as we held each other, and she asked me to marry her. I still remember the mixture of tension and delight, the joy of the moment as the breeze blew around us. When we returned to town, I told her that I wanted to consider her proposal carefully. I wanted to have some sense of certainty in my heart that, having waited so long to marry, I was making a choice for life. And I wanted to be sure that if we did not have children, it would cause no great sense of loss. She loved her daughter, but I felt for some inexplicable reason that motherhood was foreign to her.

Later that night when we made love, Anna cried before falling asleep. In the creamy candle light her cheeks were flush with color, and I remembered when my mother would say in reference to her little son, *Look, Look at the roses in his cheeks*. When she said this, she roared in delight: that was one of the few memories I had of her being happy. I looked again at Anna in the candle light, at her warm face and red lips, then I rolled over and looked upwards, through the ceiling of the bedroom, up into the sky, and said, *Mom, look at her cheeks, look at the beautiful roses in her cheeks*. Mother looked down and beamed at both of us. I turned again to Anna. Her eyes were shut, her face smiling, her lips still deep red.

It pains me to speak of Anna at length. After a week of being together I took Anna, without her daughter, on a journey into southeast Utah, and then the three of us spent a month on the West Coast. The discussions of our future centered on marriage. Some hole in my center, or an immense stone, blocked me from moving forward. I have no words to explain fully what I felt and experienced then, but, looking back, I see fear at the center of my indecision. Fear that by committing to her I put myself once again in jeopardy of losing the person I most loved. I was so young and so vulnerable. We did love each other deeply, but I understood when she said she needed to strike out and make a stable life for herself and her daughter. After our few months of life together, we parted and had no contact. She returned to live in Los Angeles, and I stayed in the mountains.

• • •

The cold woke me with a dream, and I tossed with the feeling of rejection. Rejection in the present, rejection from Anna and others, and rejection from the ancient past. There in the fullness of consciousness was one looming word in visual memory—rejection—without any physical substance. And with that word came the memory that I, too, have rejected people who had wanted only a loving touch. What is the Halflife of rejection? What daughter entities does it spawn?

DESERT

The job with the architect in Santa Fe wound down as the work concluded in Socorro. I became, however, interested in learning more about the making of architecture. My parents had a passion about architecture that manifested itself in the house they designed for us in Memphis. Although as a teenager, I knew little about Frank Lloyd Wright, my parents studied his work in *House Beautiful*, and eventually our new house on Shady Glen Road reflected his organic principles. Living spaces pin wheeled around an open-sided, charcoal gray brick fireplace, and each bedroom opened onto a garden enclosed with Japanese shoji screens made of translucent fiberglass. Beautiful but austere when finished, the house became the refuge for my mother as she spent her last years here, bed ridden with cancer. Despite the loneliness of the house, it had a soul and an aesthetic, so at the end of the mourning years in Santa Fe I set out traveling to see Wright's architecture, ultimately arriving in Arizona at his home, Taliesin West, where Wright's widow and disciples still lived and worked.

Led by the widow of the famous architect, the commune I found was rich in character and complexity. Calling themselves Fellows, some members were morosely quiet, others relentless talkers, some were twisted, others dull, and all of them lived under the matriarch's spell. Ritual defined the life of the commune. A bronze bell at the main complex rung daily at six o'clock in the morning to announce breakfast. I walked every morning along a path through the desert, watching for horny toads, lizards, rattle snakes, and javelinas, who remained, heard but invisible. We ate hearty breakfasts in the dining room, the same faces every morning, all awake and ready to work so early. To our jobs we then went—the draftsmen to their boards and me to the archives to work where all Wright's drawings lay in wide metal files.

The bells rang again mid-morning when all stopped work and gathered for coffee, tea and baked scones or cookies. Work then resumed until the lunch bells when the Fellows reconvened. A retreat followed lunch, a nap for some, a break during the heat, but the work resumed by three o'clock. Another tea break followed in late afternoon, and at seven o'clock the bells announced dinner, which required some preparation – cleaning up, a change of clothes, a heightening of formality. Bruce, my host and head of the archives, rarely attended as he had become one of Mrs. Wright's servers. Being a personal waiter was a high honor for him, a position of esteem and status in the commune.

The weekends varied the ritual life. The bells rang, but Saturday morning was devoted to cleaning and tending the property. Everyone had assigned tasks: vacuuming, window washing, and of great importance, replenishing the flower arrangements and setting the tables for the Saturday Evening, the social culmination of the week. Since a requirement to live at the compound was ownership of a tuxedo or formal dress, everyone dressed up for the Evening.

The event began with lighting of the glazed ceramic Chinese dragon outside the Wrights' private quarters. Blasts of gas flame shot from its mouth as the creature, dormant during the day, came to life at night. When the bells rang, we all entered the Wrights' living room where the senior members of the fellowship served us, along with special invited guests. Eschewing black tuxedos, many of the Fellows had colorful dinner jackets – green, maroon, or patterned black and white so the resemblance to happy parrots was inevitable. When the Saturday Evening took place in winter, a fire roared in the living room. At a fixed moment after the start of cocktails, Mrs. Wright entered from her quarters with her entourage, which consisted of two twin sisters, who were personal assistants, a private secretary, and her own physician, who was rumored to be her lover. At another preordained moment cocktails ended, and all proceeded to dinner. The feast moved depending on the season. Sometimes we dined on the covered terrace where we had most meals, or on special occasions we ate in the cabaret, a semi-submerged theater made of desert stones and concrete, festooned on the inside with tiny lights and fir boughs. The tables in the cabaret ingeniously folded down to make banquettes so that after clearing the dishes, the place was instantly reconfigured as a theater where every Saturday we watched a movie.

• • •

Bruce's house where I stayed was a place of circles, consisting of four cylinders of different sizes located carefully on a gridded red concrete pad. Wright had designed the house for another site in California, but Bruce and his father had built it there in the desert in the 1970s. Located far to the southeast of the compound, the walk to it wound through the desert with mountains to the north and an immense vista to the south of the valley whose desert edge had only a few houses and no trace of subdivisions. Passing over a gravel auto court through a metal gate strung with bells, a visitor entered between a large drum on the left, containing the main bedroom, and two smaller drums on the right that encompassed a circular kitchen and guest room. The view beyond the entry led to a terrace shaded with a trellis and the largest drum that held the living room with its fireplace, baby grand piano, banquette seating along the wall, stereo system, and television.

Circles within circles in horizontal and vertical planes, the house was a marvel. A great circle subsumed the drums themselves and within the outermost circumference lay the arc-shaped pool in which we often sat, naked, drinking gin and tonics. Ribbon windows, located at eye level and limited in height to a foot, controlled the views from the interiors when sitting. When standing, a visitor saw the room's interior, yet was protected from the withering Arizona sun, but once seated within any of these circular spaces the windows at eye level provided panoramic views. Through these slivered openings the stars sparkled at night.

Snakes dominated my first memories of the desert compound. I saw my first great rattle snake in late afternoon at Bruce's house. Clearly uncomfortable on the grass, it undulated onto the gravel near a parapet wall that flanked the small swimming pool. The snake slid back and forth along the wall looking for an opening to the desert beyond. Having informed Bruce of our visitor, I watched with binoculars when he sprayed the snake with a hose. Instead of moving away, the rattlesnake headed for the source of the water. We retreated to the house. For hours the snake moved back and forth along the side of the wall by the pool, occasionally resting in a flowering Bougainvillea. Then at once, the snake arched itself and went straight up over the wall, just above a large, slow jumping frog.

A second rattler appeared later the same day. I was lying naked by the pool in the heat of the late afternoon and heard movement in the gravel. Four feet away the serpent moved against the wall like his predecessor, looking for a way out. It followed the same routine of moving against the wall, resting in the Bougainvillea, and finally, moving, erect, over the parapet.

• • •

The desert was full of life. Mice, lizards, and horned toads skittered among the rocks. Cactus wrens, red cardinals, and hawks flicked across the green saguaro cacti and mesquite bushes. Everything living was sensitive to the slightest moisture. After a rare night of rain, the shadows of the woody trunks of the cacti appeared black. Against the green-black an evanescent cushion of fuzzy needles bloomed with the faintest vermillion, and red spines emerged from the barrel cactus. The air filled with wet desert smell. All life woke in the moisture of the winter coolness.

Bruce told me one morning that he dreamt the guest room, where I was staying, was full of snakes. Everywhere they writhed slowly in unison. In his dream, one of our friends screamed into the room that this was the one day in the year that the snakes moved in slow motion because they were preparing to mate. Bruce replied to the friend that he was terrified at the sight of the snakes. He awoke, went back to sleep, and continued to dream of snakes.

My dreams were equally strange. My dead mother appeared one night. She so rarely entered a dream that I sat up in bed to see where I was. Perhaps she was visiting the son she had left so many years ago. Sometimes the nights were too full of dreams to sleep. One night I felt that a volcano exploded in my brain. Every two hours I sat upright and felt a lava flow of burning images, one after another, of terror and angst, of death itself. On the following night the dreams were rampant again, detailed, and intense in color.

· · ·

The memories of my father walked by my side on many strolls though the desert. After his first seizure, when we still hoped for a full recovery, I visited in the hospital, but all he said was *as you get older, you have fewer and fewer friends, fewer and fewer dreams*. That last time I saw him, he sat in his bed rotating his right hand drawn into a fist. The inoperable tumor in his brain pressed on the nerves controlling the hand, and he quietly fought against losing use of it. No words then. He only looked at me with his blue eyes and communicated abstractly: *this is how it ends, this is how it ends*. I cannot parse the feelings his face communicated: sadness, anger, pain, resignation—the words are all too vague. In those moments my heart broke in two, slowly and silently. Within three weeks my father died at home. He had chosen to stop chemotherapy and had left the hospital, feeling it removed any dignity from his dying. I had so wanted to be with him as he moved towards death, but my cousin, his business partner, and my father's second wife had forbidden me to see him. A year earlier I had announced to them all that I would not enter their family business, that I would pursue art. My father responded unexpectedly with a mixture of anxiety and disapproval. If I chose the path of art, he announced, I would be henceforth cut off from all support. I could pursue my journey, but I must pursue it alone. The stepmother, who was always jealous, enjoyed this castigation, and the cousin, who craved control and domination of others, decided on a long term retribution in a plan he would effectuate for many years as the executor of father's estate.

The rupture with my father was neither ugly nor bitter but cold and hard. He seemed to have always supported my love of art, of making objects, and had never suggested I take over a business for which I had not been well suited. I did not then understand why he was punishing me. I did not comprehend the nature of his anxiety. My only wish was to reconcile with him, to obtain his approval, to calm his anxiety. I had offered to come to Memphis and help in the family business while father recovered, but the three of them said I could come only if I committed to work permanently. Torn deeply, I declined the business this second time, and the expulsion ensued: I was no longer allowed to visit. But I did see my father that one last time, on my twenty-second birthday as he turned his fist in circles. His Halflife extinguished, this good man died after 54 years of life.

• • •

The rhythm of the life in the desert soothed me and, escaping my own pain, I enjoyed listening to others' stories. Gradually, each day allowed one more small improvement at the archives as we preserved Wright's beautiful drawings and organized his voluminous correspondence. A self emerged that felt the Halflife of loss, but stood apart. Hours passed as I worked at my round table, feeling the light turn the world into three dimensions, then flatten it at mid-day, and return material to form through the shade of late afternoon. Days, weeks, months passed in ritual and rhythm. The stillness entered me slowly. I had found a place of refuge.

• • •

At the end of winter the matriarch of the commune died and went to ashes in her eighty-second year. Her followers wandered forlorn, looking about them at the sloping plane of the desert and its encroaching suburbs. I thought often of my friends and how the loss affected them. The matriarch guided their lives. Now there would be no more gifts, like the small Swiss army knife she gave me at Christmas, no more clothes, no more instructions about who to marry and when. Who will steer their ship? The night she died, a gas oven blew up in my face. A ball of flame rushed up my chest, burning my sweater, cheeks, forehead, eyelashes, and hair. I ran to the mirror and saw and smelt a stinking, brown-grey cobweb of singed matter stuck to my face. The blisters and cornea problem came later.

• • •

THE BAY AREA

Rootless again, I looked for a place of solidity, a place of belonging. My travels crisscrossed the country, gyrations that allowed few possessions: an intarsia box that my grandfather had given me, the baby tooth cast in a small wafer of clear resin from my dog Minnie, a small brass ampoule with drops of the fragrance Rain from Kiehls pharmacy, a necklace of blue Venetian beads, and a fold of purple velvet. During the travels when I settled for a few days or weeks, I unfolded the purple cloth and laid out the objects on it. They constituted a moveable private ark, objects for a retablo, symbols of home.

The folding and unfolding of cloth ended when I arrived in San Francisco with Merlin, the truck, and Minnie, the dog. By good fortune I found a store front for rent on Powell street in an area of Italian North Beach known as Little Sicily. The widows of the fishermen still swept the sidewalks in front of their immaculate cottages, and pruned and watered their geraniums with care.

The store front, empty for some time, faced Powell Street and opened at the rear onto a garden. Below, the basement held a Kung Fu studio and above were apartments. A neighbor informed me that a Chinese magician had formerly lived in the space. He must have departed hurriedly as he left behind a pair of wands and only his calling card, announcing Tai King Lee, Wonder-Man of the Orient. I peeled the newspapers off the storefront glass to open a space for the display of objects. Sometimes the vitrine held a vase of flowers, or a single chair, or, once, a large brass bird cage. At night I pulled down a white translucent screen behind the display and projected images onto it from the rear with a slide projector. Nocturnal strollers saw a constantly changing array of images. In daytime, passersby could see beyond the display to the long narrow space where I worked. Beyond it, hidden from view, were three rooms to the side. In one room I set up a bed, in another, tables for making sculpture, and in the third, a kitchen with a Roper six-burner gas stove, refrigerator, sink, and bathtub raised onto a white lacquered base.

At auction I bought a walnut ship's post office made in the 1820s. Basically, a big box with cubby holes still labeled with alphabetical letters, it became the repository of fetishes, love letters, locks of hair, delicate cups and saucers, a sewing awl, iridescent feathers, and certain magic objects. On top of the cabinet I placed the intarsia box and objects that had traveled with me. It reminded me of the pious, shuffling grandfather, and it still held the dog's tooth, the brass ampoule, and the blue beaded necklace. Like everything connected to my grandfather, the intarsia box was a mystery. I assumed it came from Russia as his parents had, but the only traces of family origins lay in the letter he wrote me just before dying. A diabetic with deformed feet, my grandfather was gentle, taciturn, and sad faced. He visited us at most once a year, so I knew little of him though I was eager to learn more. He never spoke of the past nor did my father, as if a covenant between them prevented any mention of the family life they must have shared. The ban extended to every aspect of my father's life; many people considered his muteness a sign of stoic strength.

To furnish the storefront further I retrieved the sole objects of my past, the weavings and a few other items, that had avoided the flames. Made when I was thirteen and fourteen under the direction of Henry Easterwood, my weaving teacher in Memphis, they consisted of a large tapestry of an abstracted landscape, a wall hanging we called Fuschia Garden for its intense reds, pinks, and oranges, a smaller tapestry, again of abstracted natural forms, and an unfinished rug of long, deep blue tufts. Two woven pillows had also survived. But one other tapestry was lost as it had been located in my father's office which had closed and its objects dispersed. I also had retained an album of family photographs and a box of medals. The photographs were particularly important as they included a half dozen images of my mother. Two snapshots showed her smiling as she tended vegetables in what must have been a victory garden during the war. Her dark curly hair wrapped in a kerchief, she wore a loose dress with a dotted pattern and was bending close to the earth tending sprouts of carrots. In the other photos, taken later, her face was often pained, her figure bloated. The medals testified to my father's prowess as a great runner. In high school and at Yale he had been a track star of serious talent and destined for the Olympics of 1936. I never knew why he did not participate, and he never explained. Did being a Jew keep him from Berlin the year that Jesse Owens ruined Hitler's dreams of Arian triumph?

• • •

I knew only one person when I arrived in San Francisco, and a friend of his kindly took me on as an apprentice in the restoration of furniture. The friend's friend had majored in chemistry in college but dropped out to work for his brother restoring antiques. Instead of waiting on tables I began to make a very modest living through the work of my hands. Shaping, sanding, and smoothing old and worn objects of wood seemed so natural that hours passed in the work. Attaining proficiency, I soon left my master, opened my own shop in the storefront, and found clients. Within a short time sundry chairs of all shapes and sizes came through the studio; elaborate Victorians with curved backs and elegant subtle Queen Annes, as well as Louis XIV and XV chairs, ottomans, and occasional secretaries. Tables, desks, chests on chests began to appear—all needing the touch of the hand.

The work meant breathing life into battered wood, restoring the glow to layers of worn varnish, carving a missing volute, shaping a molding to match one cut with a wood plane—anything that brought back life. For the most shimmering luster, I used French polish, a technique of hand-applying shellac in a controlled series of figure eights, circles, and linear strokes. The constant movement pushed the polish deep into the pores of the wood so that light reflected through multiple layers of finish. The final layer was burnished to produce a surface that no machine could match. Everything depended on the hands, especially the finger tips.

The work progressed so that the tips could sense the slightest variation of surface change and texture. The touch released deep memory in the woods: in Cuban mahogany, now extinct, cherry cut from trees whose girth no longer exists, and walnut with figures resembling ancient spirits locked into its wavy grain. Just as the fingertips could detect any variation, the eye taking in the surface at a low angle in the right light could see how uniform the surface became. Sometimes the work involved restoring a mahogany chest of drawers, matching fine bits of pear wood inlay, adding a delicate molding around a drawer facing, finding in my collection of old hardware a match for a solid brass teardrop pull. Or the work could involve restoring an octagonal rosewood table from the third quarter of the nineteenth century, a table made of thick veneers from an immense tree. Stored for decades, moisture had bubbled the surface, and careless feet had scratched and beaten the table's central base. After restoration, the table glowed as it had the first day it was finished in its cabinet maker's shop.

Sometimes the clients and their objects were odd. Once a man, very formally dressed and rather nervous, came into the studio. He asked if I restored trunks. I said that all depended, could he show me the trunk. He went to his car and returned with a small hump-backed trunk, painted green and clad with leather straps and wooden and brass detailing. A series of faded decals, some half falling off, covered the front and sides. *Could you restore this*, he asked? I felt expectation in his voice and saw emotion in his face. *Yes, of course. Come back in three weeks.* I cleaned the trunk thoroughly, restored the leather with several coats of emollient, and carefully repainted the green enamel in areas that had lost their surface. The decals, which had the names of an ocean liner, were glued back onto the trunk's surface and then carefully sealed with lacquer to prevent any further deterioration. The decals all came from the same ocean liner, and must have been applied at the same time. While most of the work in the shop consisted of fine antiques, many of museum quality, as well as rare artifacts, the trunk stood out, glowing somehow as if it contained its own story. Often I thought about it and eventually realized that the gentleman who had brought it was of Italian ancestry and this was the very trunk that he had taken with him when, as a young boy, he emigrated from Italy to the United States in the early part of the century. To him it meant a great deal. When he finally arrived to pick up of the trunk, I was touched to see not only his smile but the tears that came to his eyes.

Occasionally a decorator brought in a Chinese lacquered screen; these were the most difficult objects to restore. The dry climate of rooms shrunk the innards of the screens. Beneath the cracked lacquer lay the gray clay-like bole and linen that provided a substrate between the surface and the wood frame of the panels. Filling in the gaps between the subsurface and the outer lacquer was particularly challenging. In addition, the panels were often multi-screened with as many as sixteen panels so they were heavy and difficult to move.

Because of their proximity to the Far East, family connections, and cultural appreciation, San Franciscans retained much of their Asian art, and such objects rarely appeared in the rest of country. Consequently, I was able to work on many cases and display cabinets—Japanese tansu and chigaidana—even walls of multiple drawers used by herbalists for their wares. On one occasion I received a large Kang sofa which needed missing pieces of fret work. Its sides were frames containing insets of beautiful marble panels. The gray and white of the marble panels created the illusion of a landscape. The bed's surface, composed of very fine, tightly woven caning, was anchored by four posts that created a canopy; on its side had been cushions, now missing, where opium smokers took their delights. Re-carving the missing frets was difficult as their location was awkward and the wood into which the new frets had to be spliced was extremely hard. My body contorted to find the right angle and during the carving the razor sharp Swiss chisel slipped and cut into the joint of my index finger, nicking the tendon sheath. A smooth, deep incision produced bright red blood, and I worried about staining the caning. But this was only one of two accidents: the other had occurred when a board of Brazilian rosewood flew out of a saw and across my face, breaking my nose and putting a permanent dent above my right eyebrow. Marks of the warrior, I told myself.

• • •

Minnie, the dog, and I walked everyday to the wharves, Russian Hill, Telegraph Hill, along Columbus Avenue, or deep into Chinatown. People who knew animals recognized the extraordinary spirit within her. On one of our walks we began to notice an Indian man who, like us, took regular strolls. The dark white cotton of his robes set off the copper color of his skin. A gray beard accented his face, and he carried a walking stick with him. His carriage was erect and dignified; his gaze penetrated everything he observed. I watched him with fascination, but he never looked at me. He did look at the dog every time we passed him. Finally, one day he nodded to the dog, and I dared to speak to him. He explained he was a raga singer and guest professor at a local college. He asked no questions of me, but said: *your dog has a very, very deep spirit*. He smiled and moved on. We never saw him again.

Certain markets in Chinatown and North Beach emerged as favorites, and from them I provisioned dinners held in my studio. For a dinner party I assembled random chairs under restoration, placed them along the long work tables, and invited friends whose vocations and characters were as mixed as the chairs. Dinners were simple but copious. One night we might have tiny Bay shrimps, sautéed heads on in butter, garlic and parsley and served on bamboo trays, followed by long green beans with walnuts, a salad of arugula, and dessert of *sacre pantina*, a heavenly pastry from one of the Italian bakeries. Another night might offer crispy roasted duck from Chinatown, asparagus, endive salad, and the special gelato of the day. We laughed at these dinners as the city still lay in a joyous, sensuous rapture that AIDS had not yet extinguished.

Living and working in one place during the day prompted me to visit the cafes and bars at night. Some bars were still known only to locals. Tosca, with its dark interior and marble tables, evoked a special feeling of old Italy as opera emanated from a juke box. Occasionally some of the strippers from the clubs would have a drink there, and I befriended a couple of them, including the famous Karen Kessler. Her large breasts had made her appear to the public as the caricature of the dumb blonde sexpot, but I found the stereotype inaccurate. A vegetarian, she was healthy in every respect, gentle and perhaps even lonely though men (and women) ogled her nightly. One night I waited for her at Tosca and after a few drinks, she asked me to come home with her. Located high up in one of the tallest and newest high rise buildings, her apartment had marvelous views of the city. By 3:00 A.M. when we arrived, I could barely keep my eyes open, but she wrapped me in her arms and pressed her famous breasts into me. They were harder than I was, and we fell asleep holding each other.

Leaving after sunrise, I felt I had failed her, not by the absence of some impressive sexual prowess, but by not giving her the basic human love she deserved and needed. Seen by the world as a grotesque object, she was delicate, lonely, and warm-hearted, but I had so little emotional sustenance to give her in our ephemeral connection.

• • •

Regardless of the night's revelries in North Beach, I always woke early and began the day conversing with Minnie as we strolled the neighborhoods. Upon returning to the studio, the hands would then smooth the curving rosewood yoke of a Chinese chair or brush on another layer of varnish on a cherry side table. Work on sculpture began, spliced into the time dedicated to the rescue of old objects. I started drawing from life again and soon commenced work on a plaster torso of a twisting human figure. Once again the powder of plaster filled my nostrils and covered my hair as I worked the surface with rasps and rifflers, all traditional files that shaped form and allowed surfaces to move from rough to smooth or vice versa.

Ritual events punctuated the days and nights. A visit to the markets, a coffee at Mario's Bohemian cigar store, more work, another jaunt with the dog, and nocturnal rambling constituted a rhythm of life, a counter force to the halving of atoms in the decay of being. During these walking meditations the losses receded in a diurnal rhythm. I experienced a solitary fate punctuated with laughter and delight.

• • •

Although family had vanished, people began to enter my life, all bringing gifts of themselves, each teaching me something about how to love. One friend, Sabina, told me that people in general needed to hear the words that they are loved, and that she, in particular, needed to hear them. I understood the importance of touch, but the words had escaped me. *I need the words*, she said. She taught me about nourishing others. She made me see that people need much love, that they need to hear the words whether or not they say so. Sabina was the truest of friends, and we shared many adventures. Although living hand to mouth, she brought me little gifts as tokens of her own love and our friendship: a tiny bottle of Coca-Cola to drink after dinner, a magic box she found in Chinatown, a beautiful, fresh fish. She was also kind to all animals and knew much about nature and all matter of species, from chameleons to cats. Rarely succeeding with love affairs, she often told me stories of her breaking heart.

Another friend was an actress, Judith, who became my lover. She showed me how to nurture through small gestures. Sometimes when she saw my pain, she would say, *Let me bring you a cup of sage tea*. She would then fill the wicker tea basket with sage, pour hot water over it, and after steeping, hand it to me while I soaked in a bath. Sometimes, she would take one of her essential oils and put a drop on my forehead, or she would rub tiger balm onto my shoulders when they drew up into knots. In those days I only knew how to repay her gifts by planting myself deeply into her, to the point that my heart would overpower the conflicts of my mind, and she could feel what love I had. She too, like many of the other loved ones, is gone; her death by AIDS contracted from her husband.

Two friends on Powell Street, Norman and Chappie, loved me in their ways and taught me much. They lived inside a strange shell of a building with a broad curving roof and large display windows that were opaqued in white paint. Clearly something unusual occurred within, but several months passed before I was able to meet the two men who lived and worked inside this converted neighborhood grocery store. Norman designed furniture, applied faux finishes to objects, and occasionally created neo-classical houses for private decorators or rich clients. Chappie (his nickname for Chapman) was a master of *trompe l'oeil* painting and could recreate in casein any idyllic scene from any image as well as floral patterns, faux boiserie, moldings, and cornices. As I had developed a specialty in clear finishes, and they were masters of painted finishes, our creative work was complementary.

A visit to Norman and Chappie resonated with delight. Passing through the blank display windows, a visitor entered Norman's white studio on the right with its work tables, paint cans, a drawing board—all laid out with care but utilitarian in spirit – and passed through two double doors to enter an Italian *salone*. Chappie's studio was on the left. Beyond their studios the pair had covered every surface of the old grocery with illusionistic images, including vistas of Vesuvius from the Bay of Naples on one side, and lunettes looking into permanently blooming gardens on the other. They had assembled all the furniture from found objects or discarded projects and repainted everything in neo-classical colors, light blue, white, and pale lemon. The floors of the *salone*, the kitchen that followed, and another sitting room, had marbleized surfaces with each pattern more sumptuous than the next, from the green of Verdi Antico to shiny black marble, flecked with veins of gold, and squares of lapis lazuli. The fakeness of it all was a constant amusement to us.

Our visits late in the afternoon after work days always began with Campari and soda, and Wheat Thins. Norman chain-smoked skinny cigarettes, and both he and Chappie enjoyed their drinks. We almost never went out, which was fine with me as I loved listening to their detailed accounts of travels in Asia Minor to see the great classical sites. Sometimes they would open a folio of prints to show me some stunning ornament. Or, they would recount the latest exploits of their friend, Delfino, the decorator who furnished houses for many of the city's rich. Not only did they share their passion and love for classical art and architecture, but they showed me the secrets of making painted finishes. As a magician is loathe to reveal his methods, I refrain from divulging the details of the special techniques that made wavy graining, faux bamboo, or crackled finishes, but the results were impressive. Not only did they teach me, they encouraged my work, both in the restoration of furniture and objects, and the figural sculpture that I had resumed, and they sent me clients. Their goodness and generosity had no limits even when their finances flagged and they struggled to keep afloat. Their care and nurture was not predicated on my conforming to some standard of performance, but simply on being whatever and whoever I was.

• • •

I heard from friends that Anna had moved from Los Angeles to San Francisco. The sadness of losing her had never left me, and I had no idea of her feelings towards me, but she had married a wealthy stock broker and had launched a career as a successful museum curator. I knew they lived high up on one of the great hills of the city, but I never saw her, as more than a universe separated us. I tried to forget what we had shared, but I often thought how strange for those we love to become so distant, as if the most intimate moments of life are a dream.

Beneath the surface of diurnal rhythms, I was still alone and unsettled, and although I had made my own refuge, unrooted. I took out a fabric patch that I had left in the ship's post office, turned it over, looked at the delta at its center, and saw a single word: change. I soon began plans to close the studio and move on to some other quest.

VILLA TRICE

Abreeze blew fine graphite dust over the drawing on my desk. The scattering of gray powdered mattered little as I quickly cleaned the surface with a whisk brush. Across the desk lay the floor plan of the villa in which I lived. In a chair next to the desk sat the divorce papers I had signed earlier in the morning. With a few signatures and Judge Perkins' approval, the marriage to Helena had dissolved. A sadness hung around me, but there were no tears as the life begun four years ago had ended earlier. Her taste, her smile receded quickly.

The house we had shared was authentically Italianate, a real villa, in Texas of all places, built in 1917 after the designs of Villa Gamberia. The author of this place was a playwright and theater critic who spent summers in Italy and wanted to bring back some of its spirit in the house he designed for his newly married sister. Helena and I had moved to the villa after I had finished my graduate studies in architecture, and we both had found jobs at the university. I began to write more than practice architecture, and taught the history of architecture instead of design. I told myself that my making art, as I had from childhood onward, had transformed itself into an equivalent life as an academic, but I never fully believed this deception.

On the day the divorce papers were signed, I continued the measured drawings of the house and its landscape features. If some day the villa came to harm, the drawings would allow its restoration. By drawing it I also captured some aspect of its soul in the way that a photograph can steal into the being of a person and latch onto and preserve their core. I called it Villa Trice in honor of Lois Trice, the elderly English professor who had lived there for many years until her death.

The house sat within ten-foot high walls and extended through the block from one street to another. Entering through an arched gate of wrought iron covered with a verdigris patina, a visitor proceeded up six steps to a terrace in the middle of which was a rectangular pond oriented north south and a wide set of low brick steps. Beyond the terrace and steps lay the front door with its circular arch; bricks ran along the entire front of the house, leading to a terrace on the east side. This terrace, raised two feet above the ground, provided a perfect outdoor room: surrounded on three sides by a glazed terra cotta balustrade, a light trellis of steel pipes supported a luxurious, sprawling, and sweetly scented white wisteria. A fountain with a polychromed spout poured from the house side into a deep narrow pond. Sitting at a table on the veranda, a visitor looked over the front yard to the right and to the side yard to the left. The side yard, which was reached by two wide steps, was actually a lawn, originally for croquet, surrounded on two parallel sides by serpentine gardens backed with trees, and along the rear street by a high wall at whose center was another fountain with shallow basin. Just west of the side yard was a frail two-story wood garage. On its bottom floor was a disused area of stored odds and ends, and on its top floor, a one-room apartment. Between the garage and back door of the main house sat a service court where I planted a small vegetable garden.

Originally, I had only a few objects with which to furnish the villa. One day while unpacking the ship's post office, sent from San Francisco with all its magical fetishes, I found two unfamiliar cloth objects. One was an old book bag, stenciled with the insignia of a college. The other was a scarf of white silk. On its surface were smooth five-pointed stars that shined as if they were burnished. The stars glistened because they sat above their background and were woven in a twill. Each star had a hole in its center. I had owned the scarf for some time, yet I did not recall how I came to posses it. When it fell out of the cabinet, it was as if I had seen it for the first time. It spoke Anna's name, her soft whiteness, its stars were the ones we had seen together.

I also had sent from storage in San Francisco, the large tapestry I had made as a young teenager at art school in Memphis. Guided by the careful and gentle hand of Henry Easterwood, my teacher, I had woven an abstracted landscape. A rare survivor, mounted in a simple and battered gilt frame, the tapestry fit perfectly onto an empty wall on the side of the dining room and the opposite end of the French doors that opened onto the terrace.

• • •

The Halflife of marriage is an elastic measure, so short between Helena and myself, four years of furious radioactive decay. I doubted that we two were the only people with emotional voids, drawn together by the warmth of two sticks rubbing together in the hope of creating a flame. Looking again at the divorce papers, I reflected how I had betrayed her by never letting go of Anna, but that letting go was not a matter of choice. And often I thought I did not love Helena adequately. She had her own deep fixations, her own unsevered connections. Abused as a young teenager by her stepfather, she doubly suffered. First, her victimization had turned her into a secret child bride, an object of insane adulation. And secondly, she suffered loosing the abuser, when finally exposed and exiled to South America, where he vanished. Grandiose on one hand, seared through her heart on the other, I neither knew this history, nor finally learning of it, could do anything to comfort her, change her, or reach her. Perhaps she had loved me as best she could, but my needs were too great, my own loss too marked by the accelerated rhythms of loss and death.

I realized in the failure of marriage I shared a bond with many others. My journey of feeling was not so different from those of my friends. Anger and resentment led to disappointment. Where once there was desire and passion, regret melted into sensations of nothingness. I thank her for what she did provide in her own way. Yes, she did love me, we did share a life however briefly. I regret I could not love her more deeply.

As I looked from my desk at the villa over the pond and wrote the words about Helena, I observed, as I had many times, but never spoken or noted, that my handwriting resembled that of my mother. Somehow I had absorbed her peculiar scrawl, not through genes, but through a visual osmosis. Since she had written me few letters when I was away, this absorption must have come about from seeing her hand writing on some items she identified as mine when I went off to camp. She placed my name on a little cardboard sewing box so it would not get lost and on a few other items. And she had made certain my name was sewn into the fancy overcoat I took to boarding school. In those efforts I realized that she had cared for me and in rubbing her hands through my dark curly hair, she not only delighted in the son she had brought into the world, but had affirmed him deeply in a single moment of joy and laughter. Our shared handwriting, however, resembled the scratchings of a madman.

• • •

Moisture often hung in the air at Villa Trice, but before the sun's full vaporization of the clouds began, the air could comfort. When the big heat came, it made me mad, rendering my thoughts random. Only the wet heat causes such madness. It softens some part of the mind and occludes whatever allows the mind to focus, as if the lens within is made cloudy. Maybe it melts a waxy connector between consciousness and unconsciousness or an internal bridge of tissue over which electrons flow. If the bridge is severed, the electrons spill out chaotically, randomly floating throughout the body.

During one heat-induced ramble, I studied the effects of spitting cherry pits into a clear glass of water. After a few minutes, the clear water became slimy, the pits, fuzzy bald heads shaved haphazardly to leave thin tufts of red hair, like hair on the head of a clown. A nectarine pit had a different effect in water; dropped into the glass, it made a yellow film and sprouted fibrous tentacles from its prickly, russet body. On another ramble, I considered how Halflife's decay proved relevant for the body politic as I read that New York's mayor had announced unusual amounts of plutonium had been found in the city's water supply. Reassuring the citizens that there was no need to worry, he said the amount was only twenty times the normal level of phentocuries that entered water in all the above ground nuclear testing over twenty years. All references to the Halflife of plutonium were politely omitted; however, the mayor's office briefly mentioned plutonium's facility in causing bone cancer. After a few weeks the city would forget about the plutonium in its water as its presence became a fact of nature and other global calamities distracted the citizens.

• • •

At the villa a light in the aftermath of thundershowers could produce a deep hue of green from the gardens. The water lilies in the front pond passed through their own cycles of Halflife. Starting in the spring, their stalks and leaves doubled in area within a short time, and they began producing daily flowers of white, pink and peach petals with saffron yellow stamens at their centers. Some lilies crouched on the water's surface, others shot up on stalks. The blooms lasted three to four days then receded under the water's surface, waiting for their successors. With the summer heat, the larger leaves began to burn at the edges. Even the young leaves crinkled and shriveled. Twisting out of the water, they fell to the surface and began to rot. The decay was so extensive that its floating mass could solidify the whole pond. Beneath this organic homunculus at the bottom of the pond the water was cool.

On one morning during the growing season a single large white flower bloomed at the edge of the lily patch— no other blooms emerged that day. The blooming lily had a perfect symmetry and pure whiteness. It stood with a rectitude and balance upon the water that made the randomness of other stalks and pads appear chaotic and disheveled. Golden stamens emerged at the center of the lily's radiating white petals. Opening only with the sun, this lone lily blossom had a marked time.

I had seen other lilies in a pond maintained by the garden club, but their lilies were in pots. Each plant sent out its stalk from a central tuber, and from each tuber a blossom emerged. The pads were orderly, the blooms of yellow, pink, and white on various plants were handsome, and their pond water was clear. But at the villa pond, the pads were in chaos. None were confined by pots, and each obeyed its own rules of bloom and decay.

A wind blew through the town in the late afternoon and shook the lone lily bloom. Suddenly, it too lost its strength and followed the quotidian ritual, dipping under the surface to loose its petals and to begin its decay. As I watched the lily slip under the water, patterns of shadow and blazing clear light rhythmically rolled over the grounds of the villa. In some dark sky patch, the thunder sounded, but there was no rain. The air became charged with moisture but had no release. The humidity was oppressive.

• • •

The local landscape heated up like the rest of the world. The holes in the ozone, poked by our own pollutants, suggested an eventual conflagration. Or maybe our incineration will come from within long before the sun chars us as the primordial magma within the earth's center spews up through the rings of volcanoes encircling the Pacific Ocean. Or maybe the nuclear reactors scattered around the world will make their own unstoppable, excoriating flow. If the fires within crush and incinerate the globe, the remaining cinder will only be hot and inert. If the pus of nuclear fission spreads, the globe becomes a poisoned, floating tumor. In both cases, this planet is inconsequential in any galactic frame.

While working on the drawings of the Villa I sometimes drew with only one eye opened. Without the benefit of my glasses, I saw better with one eye than two. One eye looked inward, the other outward—a crazy scrambling went on inside the brain to make sense of the world. In the right eye, a virus rested that at any inauspicious moment could erupt and creep over the cornea leaving lesions in its wake and the potential for blindness. Three times this virus has erupted, usually after a high fever. I remembered this enemy within, and wondered if James Joyce also suffered from *Herpetic Keratitis*. Wandering around Trieste with a patch over one eye, his agony must have been intense. Photophobic with the white of his eye turned blood red, he risked permanent blindness. No miracle drugs existed then to combat the virus, but the cornea could be scraped with a scalpel to remove the occluding lesions that looked like tiny tunnels dug into the eye's surface. This virus, like an addiction, is never cured and only waits for some vulnerable moment to burst forth, filling our cells with confusion and polluting our neural synapses, changing our behaviors and dependencies.

The fragility of the body reinforces the hurtling force of Halflife. One knee has been swollen for months with fluid, and I limp around feeling one side of my leg hotter than the other. I cut off the tip of a finger while pruning the exuberant lantana. The tip grows back, but the nerve does not, so a mute mound of skin sits where sensitive ends once felt the texture of clay and the subtle ripples of a planed board.

• • •

Jay, a young, spirited designer of much talent, was a colleague at the university and friend. Once, he asked me to the gym with him. He had AIDS and wanted to see if he liked exercising in semi-public. He still had some strength, so he tried pushing his skinny body to strain against the machines. Only the day before he had told me of his not being well, although mutual friends had informed me long before we ever met. He said he feared that people would see him as having a stigma, but his skin showed no marks.

In the shower I could sense his own subtle feelings of shame, of uncertainty of his being and his body. A natural pride in a happy sexuality had been gravely damaged. Aside from the thinness of his body, he looked no different from anyone else. His sex had the character of any man's sex. Yet within, in the gametes of his seed was lethal corruption.

How mad can life be that human seed is poisoned? Creamy semen that first appears as drops of pearls at the end of a boy's penis became now the unguent of death. Liquids from all wet body places and blood itself contain the viruses that destroy women and children. The life force commingled with an insidious plague punishes the addict, the lover, the hemophiliac, the innocent child, everyone. Why has life been reduced to such an explicit and painful metaphor? Adding to our living with the possibility of total annihilation, eons of poisonous decay from our militant suns run amok, and the capriciousness of death itself, is the corruption of the life force in seed and blood. Though we want to live in the darkness of denial we are all touched by this contamination.

Seed, half the regenerative fertilizing force of life, has become poisoned. Retain seed because it transmits AIDS, because it causes pregnancy, because it puts hearts at risk. Women and men live in the fear of seed, saliva, mucous, and tears. Ova sit in the darkness of the womb waiting for infection instead of fertilization.

After Jay told me of having AIDS, I thought, *yes I know, and I will lie next to you on your death bed, listening, and be your friend and care about you, and one day I will watch you die. I imagine the grimace on your face when you know there is no return, and I will weep for you.*

• • •

By a stroke of luck I finally found the address of Henry, my old weaving teacher whom I had not seen since I was a teenager. A friend told me that he was still alive and residing in Memphis. This delicate man, thin and pale, was the other father in my life from the age of twelve to fifteen. His gentle mark formed some of what I am.

I wrote my dear teacher: *One wonders what puts people in contact after decades, but despite the many, many years since I last saw you, I have thought of you often. Always those thoughts were full of warm memories and more appreciation than can be expressed for the many things you taught me, your generosity, kindness, and, yes, affection. I ran into Larry T., our mutual friend, and he gave me your address, so I decided I should finally try to find you. Apparently, you have been in Memphis all those years while I have wondered about the globe, orphaned a bit too early, but now pretty happily settled. I am including a photo so you can see the man that grew from the boy. A man at Halflife, but still young spirited and energetic.*

In all these years there is much too much to condense in a letter. I can tell you of many memories connected to you, from handling beautiful skeins of Paternayan yarn to spending blissful hours at the loom to savoring the bread-and-butter pickles you served with sandwiches. I remember the story that you chauffeured your father around in a big car as he inspected roads his company had built around Atlanta. I remember vividly the little stone house, the first place of built magic that I ever knew. I remember the fabrics and furniture and your supremely good taste. But most of all I remember your kindness in teaching me and providing a kind of guidance that my own father never could. For all those things and many more, I now finally have the chance to thank you profoundly.

Please feel free to call on me if you need anything. Your home is not so far from mine, and having crossed this chasm of decades, it only seems right to be in touch.

Henry replied, and we made plans to me meet at some point in the future.

• • •

The walls around the Villa were disintegrating gradually, and I spent some mornings repairing them, laying stone upon stone. Sometimes I strolled about the walled precinct looking for a cool, quiet place to sit. Inside, at my desk, I might select from the List of Lists, the repository of all tasks, some mundane piece of business to transact. While tending to those details one morning, friends came for a visit. A newly married couple, they began talking not about their own plans, but about the warming of the universe. Full of optimism, they saw a world of all possibilities with cures at hand. I tried to explain a darker view directed towards the world of men in general, not at individuals who retain some power for salvation. In the world, whose Halflife was accelerating, choices existed: hope, resignation, suicide, or struggle.

One chooses struggle, the other, hope, I suggested. After the friends departed, I thought to myself: embrace human life, connections, and simple observation. Embrace these things while there is time. In the struggle to embrace there is salvation. Few people talk about salvation outside the conventions of religion, but salvation is worth considering in a serious life.

In the Sunday newspaper a writer published a chart of global poisons, their causes, cures, and effects. Strangely, the long simmering poison of nuclear decay was absent from the list. Is the cellular holocaust that nuclear poison brings too gruesome to be part of everyday discourse? Edwin Teller, the hawkish physicist, raved about the benefits of nuclear reactors for bringing electricity to millions of people in India. Electricity eased human suffering, did it not? However, because we have no viable solutions for the permanent disposal of nuclear waste, fusion is a holocaust in the making, with ovens of cremation as large as cities. Imagine a substance on the tip of your finger that will burn for twenty-thousand years and kill everything in its path. Does a little tenderness between human beings soothe the burning wound?

• • •

For a place in the city Villa Trice, pond and the blooming vines, supported a surprising throng of birds and wildlife: green herons, hummingbirds, Gulf Coast toads, cats, raccoons, and possums. How wonderful it would have been to speak their languages. If that ever came to pass, I planned to hang out a sign on the garden wall:

Welcome to Doctor Doolittle's
People think we do a little, but we do a lot.

After placing the sign I would open a small treatment room inside the Villa and a repair shop out back. Not only would we talk to animals and treat them when sick, but we would fix broken objects and restore tired artifacts. A placard would announce:

Innerforms Ltd.
We fix everything but a broken heart,
And we will try to fix that too!

• • •

A slight breeze in early morning sometimes made me hope that the heat would not overwhelm me as it had the day before. The thermostat within the body was delicate and temperamental, and if unbalanced, power surged erratically like lunging water in a storm-filled arroyo. But in times of calm I enjoyed feeling the walnuts, half-eaten by squirrels, under my feet on the terrace, I listened to the birds, I ran my hands through the water at the fountain of the pond. I thought about Anna, and the friends I love. Calm and agitation vacillated inside me.

A particularly breezy morning brought whirling leaves and thoughts of fall. Even though the day had its heat, burning everything in the sun's path by mid-afternoon, a touch of coolness appeared. A simple breeze gave relief from heat and with that relief, comfort and hope.

Long ago Krishnamurti described in *The Flight of the Eagle* how the mind is the source of longing, and that thought, having experienced pleasure, wants to experience that pleasure again and again. Since no two moments are ever the same, the satisfaction of a desire is never as it once was. From this difference pain arises. A moment of joy can never be precisely experienced more than once. But I think longing may have many objectives: to feed a mouth that was never properly nourished, to redress an absence of tenderness, to connect human beings so two souls make a third. The overlapping of souls creates a gel, a transparency through which a different hue of light passes as if blue and yellow diaphanous disks were superimposed to make green. This adding of hues to make another color is the humanness of union. The white light of nature is already whole and reveals its spectral colors only when refracted through a prism or a crystal or through layers of polarized molecules.

• • •

In the mind, or heart, or some interior place that had no name, I had the sensation at Villa Trice that more time passed than was counted by days, and that days corresponded little to the units of psychological time. What is the measuring rod of psychological time? A year, a lifetime, a Halflife, a geological eon? Is it the psyche's days that weigh on us as our cells hurtle towards oblivion, that pressure and pain us as we confront all the incomplete work, the unfinished figures, the abandoned projects, the unpublished books, the untranscribed poems, the unmeasured plots, the untilled soil?

I only knew that much time passed, that the passing brought an emptiness, but also another growing season. The cooler weather allowed the roses to bloom. Light green leaves emerged from the ivy and from the potted jasmine by the door. The Impatiens burst with flowers, and the zinnias (planted late) produced magenta blooms. A pair of cardinals remained, along with three or four blue jays. Fall was gentle at the villa, winter came late.

The cleaning of the pond, the subsequent clearing of the water, and the cooler weather revealed fish swimming in schools. Two of the large speckled koy were missing, and since there have been no corpses, I assumed the green heron ate them. They could have been suffocated by large frogs who held their gills shut, but I do not believe that happened. One night I heard a splash in the pond, but when I went to the bedroom window I saw nothing but a small mystery.

• • •

My friend with AIDS, Jay, died. I now realize that the last time he had come to visit me at the villa, he had come to say good-bye. He told me his legs ached, and he was tired of the pain. After he went into hospital, I wanted to go see him, but his sister, who remained his companion and nurse, said he did not want visitors. He had been proud of his handsome looks and did not want his friends to see the emaciated skeleton he had become. The dead Jay soon visited me in a dream. Sitting rigid and straight, he drove a car to the house where I was. He said, *Help me out of the car, I cannot move my eyes*. He then asked me what I thought of so and so, a name I cannot recall. I said that I had no opinion. He then said that no funds were coming to him and to his sister and that so and so was siphoning off the funds. I told the specter that I would take care of the situation, and that if there were a problem I would give his sister anything I had.

On the morning after the dream I encountered a street person by the old garage in back of the villa. Tall, dressed in white with her head wrapped in a white turban, she asked if I could bring her a cup of coffee. When I brought her the coffee along with milk and sugar, she poured five tablespoons of sugar into the cup. Her name was Raquel, and she started sleeping in the garage among the stored items. She would spend two or three nights in the garage and then disappear for a few days. One day a wind storm descended from the northwest cracking branches in the town and signaling the long delayed arrival of freezing weather. The wind blew down the mattresses that Raquel had used to close the open end of the garage. The fallen mattresses made a strange site, as if during the demolition of her little house its facade had been peeled away. There inside was her bed carefully made with sheets turned down. The blankets I gave her were neatly folded on a box, but next to the bed were piles of refuse, mostly paper products from fast-food meals and wadded up tissues scattered about. All the cloth for swaddling her head and the white paper made her hovel monochromatic. I returned to the house and worried that she would be cold that night as the temperature approached freezing. I returned in the morning, but her bed was still made. I never saw her again, but someone claimed to have seen her shortly thereafter with one arm in a sling.

• • •

Time kept passing in units without names, and winter dissolved into an early spring at the villa. My father, who died long ago, still returned to my dreams. In those dreams he moaned and said nothing, and I could not begin a conversation. Was I too shocked by this specter, or did I not know what to ask or say? Talking with the dead in dreams is not as grim as it sounds.

I woke in the middle of the night to see clouds rake over the moon's face with swift, relentless, and translucent prongs. By morning a beautiful heavy fog covered the trees and houses. Spots of light diffused to make this familiar location seem as if all was transported to an unrecognizable place. The moisture soothed the skin of my face. When I went out to pick up the newspapers, I looked back and saw the light in my library so I knew I was still at the villa. Enjoying the fog, I thought it is good to ask what sustains us. Dancing, poetry and human touch sustain us. People live for so long without sustenance that they forget its existence – if they ever knew. Dancers must have their bodies for sustenance but they can lack words. Poets must have their words but can forget their bodies. Those nurtured by touch may never know dance or poetry, but touch sustains them.

• • •

With the full arrival of spring two red-headed woodpeckers appeared. I began to pull up the invasive nut grass, remove yellowed leaves from the Mexican heather, and watch the green geckos with red throats. The pond water became clear once again as the fish gobbled up the algae. Loving the sun, the water lilies started to bloom.

No hummingbirds had yet arrived, nor had the red dragon passed by, but I knew they would come soon.

• • •

I found an incredible object as I was mounding up hardwood charcoal for the grill. Out of the charcoal bag fell a large black, leathery frog that had been totally carbonized into a frozen state. Every piece of the frog was intact. So black and still, it reminded me of the charred body of a merchant in Pompeii who tried to rise slowly from the rain of fiery ashes pouring from Mt. Vesuvius but was caught for eternity. A frog has been turned perfectly into black charcoal. What next: will the sky rain locusts and the pond turn to wine?

• • •

Write, I tell myself. Write something. Make words on paper a life line. Then in this immense barrenness of words an idea came to me: forget the words, make places, places of refuge. Use sculpture and drawings to make places of peace and shelter. A clue appeared about how to begin: follow one strand of memory and others will appear. Out of memories images will take concrete form with one form leading to another. The composite of those images will describe the first refuge. Having made images and form for the first refuge, others will follow.

Despite the humidity that loomed through the day and night, a wonderful cold outdoor natural pool, Barton Springs, nurtured the town and provided a civic refuge. I realized that my pruning and watering the gardens at the villa, watching birds and smaller creatures, like color-shifting lizards, and many swallowtail butterflies were activities of refuge. Deep in the night, my dead father returned again in a dream. In the dream he met me at the hospital where I was having an operation on my knee. I was already on a gurney, looking at the row of other people waiting for their turn to be opened up, when he rushed in from the elevator. Dressed in black from head to toe, he immediately sat down. His pants and jacket glistened as if they were a supple patent leather, and he bent over to tie his tight black leather boots which came to his knees and had dozens of eyelets. I said, *Looking at you, Father, somebody might think you are into S and M.* He just kept fiddling with his laces and said nothing.

The image remained clear, the speechless father in glistening leather, kind enough to return from the dead while I had a torn cartilage fixed in my knee. In the midst of eating a chef's salad I thought about the dream and remembered that I had previous visitations from Father around my birthday. It was on my birthday many years ago that I last saw him alive. He died without me near him, without me looking into his eyes, or giving him one last hug. That was how it all ended. Now I know why he had returned: my birthday was the day after tomorrow.

· · ·

I waited all day for a sign about a story. The only news was that the mummified frog had disappeared. There was no trace of him on the white china plate on which I had carefully placed him in the storage room. What kind of creature delights in stealing the carbonized carcass of a frog? For all we know, this could be a supreme prize for a field mouse, a trophy, or sharpening stone for claws or teeth. Could the mouse be gobbling up this desiccated frog like we eat crispy fried chicken at a picnic? It was a mystery to me, but if I ever have the privilege of finding again a mummified frog, I will take better care of it, placing it under a bell jar, out of harm's way.

• • •

Although I was ambivalent about the material value of objects, losing things skewed my life. In the worse case, losing an object permanently altered my life, and such a fate happened to others. Anna once told me about losing a perfect, ebony egg and the words of her story showed that her life had been altered. An elderly Japanese man had made the egg in San Francisco, and she had received it as a gift. When held in the hand the egg calmed the body and touched a deep place within. Perfect in proportion, the surface was worn smooth to glistening by movements of the old man's hands. The egg fit into the class of objects we privately cherish, like special stones. One day Anna lost the egg. Everywhere she searched but found nothing. Eventually, while visiting San Francisco, she went to Japan Town to inquire about the craftsman. Yes, she was told, he was the one who made eggs, but he had died, and there were no more.

I lost a special set of objects, maquettes for a light sculpture laid out on small squares of Plexiglas that I only now found after ten days of looking. During that entire time my direction and purpose seemed vague and, at low moments, I felt lost as if these objects were parts of my body, inanimate but essential. I found them finally in a place I had already looked: a hinged mahogany box that acted as the overflow repository for personal pictures and snapshots. Why had I put them in such an obscure place?

I abhorred losing things: my piece of quartzite that splits light into double images has been missing for weeks. A couple of gem stones, chrysacolla and some pearly blue stones resembling frozen soap bubbles, have disappeared. One way of dealing with lost objects is to put them on the List of Lists. It included a special category for things lost, abandoned, stolen, or destroyed. Putting the names of objects on a list helped reduce the need to find them and eased their absence. Such is the power of words.

● ● ●

I assembled *memento mori* to recall objects of medieval contemplation. I looked at a picture of my father, remembered his sadness as he lay dying in the hospital, speaking to me telepathically. His gift to me was the lesson not to go into the darkness in the way he had and to find light in the days that remain. I began to notice a light came every day. Spectral colors poured over my desk, rainbow chords from Fresnel lenses I had mounted on the window. The lenses were prismatic strips of plastic, joined at their centers with a small suction cup to make a pinwheel. I had found the lens at an observatory; once stuck to a window, its fine grooves broke the light into violet, indigo, blue, green, yellow, orange, and red. The colors only lasted a short time as the sunlight passed through them, but their intensity startled me. The rainbows from the lenses poured over the white limestone of the hearth, and suddenly the stripes of violet green, yellow and magenta covered my face and filled my eyes. The light tells me the time is coming to leave the stories and to start making places of refuge. When the places of refuge are done, my work will be over.

Not long after the rainbows strafed the limestone of the hearth, two red dragon flies came to the pond. A pond maven had told me when the red dragon fly comes, the pond is balanced. The pair buzzed around the bougainvillea, then one lit on the lily called Heavenly Blue. The other looped into the water, slapping her abdomen on the water's surface. Over and over she looped and slapped the water. Their intense colors glowed orange and vermilion as if shining from within. Above the pond, beyond the roof ridge, immense white clouds grew, their edges turning dark as they swelled for the afternoon showers. The air became heavy with moisture. It enveloped me, and I heard only the wind and a buzz of gnats.

My thoughts turned to Anna whose Halflife quickly careened towards its end. Feeling weak, she underwent scans that showed a spot of cancer on her kidney. The spots spread quickly to her lungs. When she told me over the phone, I heard fear, disbelief, and courage. In my mind I imagined myself lying next to her in her sick bed, caressing what was left of her hair, running warm hands over her ravaged body. Cancer in the liver was a grim diagnosis.

Thoughts of mortality surrounded me in those days. Once, when I had gone to Los Angeles I tried to call the amazing author who wrote his own story of coming of age, a story that centered on being a closeted homosexual boy at the very same boarding school I had attended. I had wanted to call him to pass on appreciation for his words, delight in his stories, regardless of their pain, but I could not find his telephone number. Then, I read that he had died last year before my visit. How could I have imagined he had survived the increasing devastation of T-cells that he mentioned in the last lines of his book? This plague medievalizes life and turns the spirit inevitably again and again to death and suffering. Yet, every time I feel the shuddering fear of death, I see and feel the glancing beauty of morning light that strikes us who still breathe in this strange and mysterious universe.

An early breeze blew over my bare feet, the doves cooed, the cardinal chirped, and gardenias poured out their scent. The smell of a dead animal had woken me in the middle of the night. Sleepless, I went walking in the full moon and saw blooming daturas, the huge white caverns of tissue painted by Georgia O'Keefe. They sprang from scopolamine loaded roots. Eat those roots and you fly. When light finally came, I wandered into the courtyard garden and saw three sticks that provided a resting place for dragon flies. This roost was not intentional, but I saw them holding forth, their velvet red-orange bodies and diaphanous wings unmoving. Large buzzards circled over the oak trees. Later, a swarm of dragon flies moved in tight arcs above the garden. The flexible jaws opened and closed too quickly for anyone or creature to see. With eyes of million-pored radar, they found and devoured their prey. A small grey gecko climbed to the spot of the three sticks. He too lay motionless, deluded into thinking he could catch the elusive flying dragon.

• • •

I hired someone to help maintain the gardens. The gardener came from a rich family in the Deep East part of the state. They owned the Chevrolet dealership and a cotton compress. He went to Sewanee in Tennessee, majored in Latin, fell under the sway of a charismatic teacher of literature, studied ballet after he got out, had some kind of crisis, and started working for a landscape firm. The company did sloppy work – he knew their plants would not survive—and he set out on his own to cut lawns and trim edges. Married, possibly for a second time, he had four children. He loved William Burroughs and Yeats, whose poetry he recited. His sister, a debutante, went to college, came back to become an Episcopal priest, but was defrocked because she was a practicing lesbian.

One night the gardener called in mid-evening. He was drunk and asked over and over if the "field of dreams" was really going to happen. Referring to making a wildflower meadow at the villa, he was worried about raccoons rutting amongst the seedlings. He insisted I use sardines to catch them and that I should string Christmas lights in rows to frighten them because that worked at Mr. Fairchild's house. He asked me if I still liked him. *Yes, of course*, I said.

• • •

I often lay awake throughout the night at Villa Trice. On some nights I might write a few letters, work on a book review, and then lie on the daybed waiting in the blackest night for light. I waited for the light so I could go out and watch the birds arrive at the feeder, or observe the opossum fumbling at the water bowls. I waited for the light so I could feel the coolest moments of the day during a scorching summer. And while I waited, a raw pain often moved through me, the collation of my disappointments, venality, indignity, and mortality. I waited for the light, and noticed that my eyes focused less sharply from year to year.

Early one morning after the night's vigil a distant cousin called to discuss the fate of my Uncle Bill. We both were concerned about what would happen to him as he grew older and remained alone. The cousin cheerfully explained, as if describing the purchase of a new suit, that he had already made all of his own funeral arrangements. He laughed and finally said that all these details preceded his hearing two hours earlier that he had advanced prostate cancer.

• • •

The flagstone steps outside the garage door continually lost their boundaries as the grass slowly encroached. While their edges dissolved in the grass, the accumulating soil and an occasional fire ant nest, added to their obscurity. Over time they would disappear completely, so I tried to keep them whole by cutting away the grass at the edges. The grasses were, however, deeply rooted and did not come up easily. I took a screwdriver and moved it around the edges of the stone to break the hold of the grass. Finally, I hosed down the stones to clear the debris; the water puddled over them and when it drained away, a thin film of silt lay over the stones.

• • •

One morning while looking out the library window at the birds, instead of working on my lectures, I saw a beautiful fox run up and start nibbling the sunflower seeds that had spilled beneath the bird feeder. After eating the seeds, she drank at the pond, her small dark tongue darting quickly into the water. Her paws were large for her frame, her coat short from the long heat of summer. The fluffy tail of this gorgeous animal was almost as long as her body, her grace was breathtaking. A fox in my yard! A magical gift. Then, looking at me, she seemed to be trying to speak. I listened closely as the fox said: *I have come to a ready hand and generous heart, to the water bearer in the drought, to the man with seeds from the fields.* She sniffed the air and nodded her head in thanks for the seeds.

AQUIDNECK ISLAND

Winter settled over Aquidneck Island, the land of my paternal ancestors. Mostly a rocky peninsula in Narragansett Bay just east of Providence, the island had long nurtured farms even before the outburst of big nineteenth mansions in Newport. This place is where my father and his brother, abandoned at their mother's death, came to be raised by in-laws. It is an outcropping of rocks, farms, and small villages at the edge of a cold ocean, all caressed by fingers of clouds moving back and forth just as the sunlight from a sky by Tiepolo passes between clouds. From any promontory the sea, sky, and hard, worn rock are visible. Because winter is approaching, the trees have become bare, the grasses golden, and the evergreens tawny at their tips.

I have come to the island that was the place of my father's upbringing to write a book on architecture. I am staying in the house of my great uncle and great aunt, both dead after lives lived longer than those of our relatives. They defied the constrictions of Halflife. Dying well past the age of seventy, they were too distant to be a part of my small immediate family, but I liked them very much on the few occasions I had visited them as a teenager.

The family history remains fragments. In 1896, at the age of forty-nine, the great-grandfather applied for American citizenship. Formally from the domain of Czar Nicholas in Russia, he brought with him four of his five tall handsome sons. The fifth son, my grandfather, was yet to be born. No mention was made of my great-grandfather's wife, nor was there evidence that she obtained citizenship, or that her husband sought it on her behalf. One of the sons had a strange marriage. His future wife had fallen in love with one of the heirs of the Tiffany family. A marriage, however, between her and her beloved was impossible as she was Jewish. Somehow, perhaps through a matchmaker, she was wed to one of my great uncles and by him had a daughter. Married against her will, she was so despondent that she was put into the local mad house. The father told his daughter that her mother had died. The daughter spent her entire life up to the age of forty believing that not only had her mother died, but that she had no other living relatives. By chance a neighbor offered condolences to the daughter one day after her mother passed away. *Oh that can't be,* she said. *My mother died long ago. No, not at all* replied the neighbor. *I just saw the obituary in the newspaper. She has been in the asylum for the last forty years.*

Not only had this woman grown up with the delusion of having no family, but she had lived in the same town as her incarcerated mother. Her daughter, my second cousin, who related this saga to me, discovered this fact only when she herself turned forty and her own teenage daughter asked about the origins of the family. The second cousin found traces of a family who had once existed but seems to have vanished. Of the earliest Jewish families in the small New England town of Norwich, its dead occupied much space in the old cemetery. Many of them had died at a young age.

The original immigrant's youngest son, my grandfather, had a sad fate. Having graduated from a highly prestigious Ivy League university, not known for admitting Jews, he set out to practice law in the town of his birth. Bright and humble, he made such a mark that his employer recommended him as counsel to the town, a singular distinction for someone his age and religion. With the promising life of a lawyer, he married my grandmother, the daughter of Swedish Jews who had immigrated to the United States in 1880. Marrying her continued the tradition of Russian ancestors intermarrying with Swedes. She bore him two sons, my father and my uncle, but she died in her thirty-fifth year of tuberculosis. My father, then thirteen years-old and his brother, aged eight, were sent to live with in-laws.

What my grandfather did, where he went, the details of life with his young wife are unknown. He gave up the practice of law and became a social worker. I never clearly understood his decision – such things were never discussed in our family. But I have the impression that a deep religious piety and altruism moved him to serve others. Despite his piety, my grandfather had an unhappy life.

His youngest son, my Uncle Bill, grew strange without the tenderness of his mother or the sustenance and guidance of his own father. After he returned, shell-shocked from World War II, he went to live with my grandfather in Brooklyn. By this time my grandfather had remarried. His second wife was a writer and amateur painter, but partly because of my grandfather's lack of ambition, she divorced him, a rare event for Jews of that generation.

My father rarely spoke of his past on the island, but the remaining relatives remember him as a tall, handsome, athletic golden boy. Once or twice he mentioned sailing and the landmarks in the area: Point Judith, Circle Island, the beaches named by number, First, Second, and Third. I wondered if walks on the beach, near the house of his uncle and aunt, soothed his pain, if at the end of the beach, at the point where the pile of rocks blocked passage, he looked back and saw the heavy green fields of the boys' school in the distance with its neo-gothic tower cut into the azure sky. And if he saw this sky and the richness of the sea's color, how long and by what means did they soothe his loneliness?

I never knew if father's acid pain was ever neutralized. Deep inside it devoured him and, I suspected, led to his death. Upon arriving in Newport one of the first places I visited was the cemetery where his mother was buried near her parents, aunts, and uncles. With tears running down my face, I realized the day was the anniversary of my father's death many years before. Shortly thereafter, I visited my last surviving great aunt, whose husband of fifty years had recently died. She was so lonely that she asked me to sleep next to her. The mix of loneliness for human touch and the perversity of lying next to my seventy-eight year old aunt was strange.

• • •

Halflife pulled deeply as the daughter atoms sought entropy from the life force. The losses included not just the parents, homes, lovers, but friends in youth. I once knew a young woman, an artist, at the girls' academy down the street from my boarding school. By a peculiar coincidence she became my student in an art program where I taught one summer during my college years. She was strong and very attractive, full of character, sensuality, and tremendous talent. Everyone felt the goodness of her heart. I enjoyed her presence that summer and felt drawn to her. Then in the fall I heard that she had been killed in a car wreck. It was a loss that I have thought of often. There was also a handsome friend at the boarding school who was killed in a car accident after graduation. We were not very close, but he was radiantly beautiful and sweetly feminine. He had charm and wit far beyond his years. An only child of an elderly father and young wife, he must have been greatly mourned. Another friend, just out of college, contracted an incurable disease. He moved to the Caribbean to watch Technicolor moonlight over palm leaves as he wasted away. With thoughts of him come other memories of the young classmates who died too soon, all sweet and lovely youths. The pain of their lives torn from us fades, but never vanishes. These images of people I have not seen in decades returned sharply like sunlight through crystal as I sat looking out from my rented house towards the water.

Walks at the ocean soothed me regardless of the weather. On one morning haze dulled my favorite view of the tower on the hill at the boys' school, and snow and rain approached from the southwest. I found a child's shoe on the beach. Naturally small, all that was left was the leather sole. Spiral shells were scattered about; they had holes in them, tiny wounds by which one creature extracted the other for food or a temporary shelter. I saw prints of horse hoofs, and two lobster pots had washed up, one wrapped in a cloak of nylon net that shimmered in a web of translucent blues and grays. Were the knots that bind the web tied by hand? How did it feel tying nylon line all day long?

I also found a fishing lure, which I took and placed on the work table at the house. It resembled a fat white cigar cut short on the bias at one end. It had no hooks, but still had the metal eyes that connected it to its line. The white faded into a light blue; the whole was made of a hard dense foam, with visible cell structure, and cast in a mold as seen from the vestiges of flash lines. Small square, silver flecks speckled the outer surface of the lure. They must have been the flashy ingredient that attracted fish, because, surely, this lure resembled no fish, had no smell, no taste, no sex, and no beauty.

• • •

On the peaceful island of the ancestors the first fog of the winter occluded the morning sun. A mist kept me from the beach, and I sat in the living room, cup of tea in hand. The screens on the windows had drops of moisture trapped in their fine mesh. Each drop glinted in the gray light, pulling to itself all available illumination, making each drop appear brighter than any obvious light source. The glowing drops, hung on a regular grid, formed patterns that the eye put together as it searched for the pattern that exists independent of any human effort.

Days passed quickly in the brief sun of winter. One morning, the beach at low tide was missing the usual deposit of children's shoes, sneakers, and aluminum cans, but a small ray had washed up. The cold wind of the last several days had blown in a cloudless, blue sky that allowed an overwhelming, bright sunlight. At sunrise I saw the horse at the beach. The hoof prints had been there for several mornings, but I always arrived too late to see the animal. The stallion with rider galloped towards me. The sun trickled through purple clouds refracting and showering the shoots of clouds with gold and pink and turquoise light. The low angle of the sun sent washes of rose and blue over the film of water at the wave's edge. Each shimmer of color lasted for a moment until the froth of the wave rolled over and refreshed the palette. The rider galloped the horse up and down the beach until steam poured from the horse's nostrils. A man, walking a beagle, stopped to tell me that the galloping horse had been a race horse and occasionally was spooked at the beach; he disapproved of the horse running on the beach at sunrise. Never mind, I thought, because the colors, the sun, the froth, the sound of hooves were so soothing.

Two friends who came to visit at the island talked about cannibalism. Suddenly, I had an image of my mother's large breast with its aureole around her full nipple, and then I thought of her mastectomy. It occurred to me that I identified with her loss, that her suffering had become part of me. The scar I saw when I was thirteen was hideously disfiguring. The disease made her mad, but no one would ever so say so. She would scream that she had been carved up like a turkey. Not only had I been bound by the pain of rejection, but by the pain of empathy. Though some part of me hated and resented her, absorbing her pain, not just her victimization of me, had been a reality.

The next morning I awoke worn out from dreams with themes of vivid loss and violence. I put their details in notes as a kind of expiation. Whatever the losses were, I hoped that feeling loss no longer overwhelmed living or loving. I wanted to feel loss, but I wanted to leave it behind, to freshen the spirit by smiling deeply. The freshening was elusive, and, like some invisible radioactive force, loss pumped through my flesh slowly eating it away, yielding beta particles of decay.

• • •

Rare winter rains blew in waves over the island house while in the guest bedroom Mary Ann slept. We had lived together long ago when I was in college, had shared a life, but let go of each other. Or rather, I let go of her, but we had remained friends. How strange to have her in the guest room after years of sharing the same bed. She had arrived grieving the break with a man who could not return her love. Reclining on the couch, we shared stories of anger, disappointment, and pain. She appeared to me as desirable, as kind and warm as I remembered.

I missed the old bond between us. She still laughed and smiled with great beauty.

• • •

The calm that can arise after storms, after the settling of the sea, a calm so unexpected that it surprised my flesh, filled me as I sat in the upper floor study of the island refuge. The week had been full of tension, exhaustion, frustration of such pressure that I felt desperate for some release. Suddenly, an image of my father, smiling as in a dream, became part of my body. I could feel the smiling image of my father alive within me. I accepted his support, and I forgave him for abandoning me. We agreed that my compulsions were no longer required as atonement for guilt, as proofs of my validity, as justifications of being something very different from what he wanted. From this point forward, we would work together. His smiling image, within my heart, would be a strength, his still small voice, a soul's echo.

The comfort was short in duration. Within two days I awoke with the old feelings of abandonment, rejection, loneliness, and vulnerability, the boring, tedious, relentless old feelings. But their weight was lightened by a vivid dream of flying. With arms outstretched, I soared over fields, cottages, and along the water's edge. The flying combined exhilaration with fear at being high aloft. Then, I remembered that I had flown before, perhaps in other dreams or in thoughts before sleep. Suddenly I skimmed the surface of the water, entered the ocean briefly, and realized that coursing under water was an entirely new experience.

• • •

Minnie, the great dog, died. She ran onto the highway and was run over by a car. A friend from Santa Fe called to tell me that the body lay by the side of the road for two days, then the city refuse truck passed by and took her away. The death marked the passing of an evolved being contained in a dog. On a short visit from the island refuge, I had just seen her one week before when I visited Santa Fe. She wagged her torso she was so happy to see me. First, I washed her in a metal tub, then groomed her fur with a shedding comb and removed the thick winter undercoat with my fingers. I scraped the plaque off her teeth and took her to the veterinarian for a check-up and shots. The heart murmur was no better or worse than two years before, but the shining coat indicated good health. We went to the land in the country, the rocks where she was born, walked the fields where she had chased rabbits many times and where she had guarded me when I slept in the open. She was fierce and protective, but thunder always terrified her as if its sounds were those of guns echoing through the river canyon where she was born, each peel a shot pointed at the legs of an errant valley dog. She was also afraid of being abandoned. Her eyes would fill with sadness whenever I left her in Santa Fe, and each leaving pained her. At the end of my last visit she chased the car down the street. This I had never seen. My heart leaped in a panic as cars approached in differ-ent directions. Finally, she stopped running and stood in the street. A car slowed, she headed home. A dog who was too smart to risk traffic, who would sit at a street corner when asked, was not careless in dying. She had escaped death twice before. Once, she jumped out of a third story window because she feared being left behind when we were changing apartments. Later, an incompetent doctor pulled a molar and could not get her blood to stop flowing. He claimed it would not clot, and she spent five days in intensive care, but recovered.

Perhaps the terror of thunder drove her into the path of a car. More likely, her death was a suicide as she confronted the loneliness of living without her master who had just left her once again. Thirteen years old, in dotage and abandoned, she decided that the contentment of the last visit was final. She chose her moment and rushed on to a brief, bone-cracking end. So marked the end of a dog whom I loved very much, a dog who touched my heart and was a devoted friend. The grave spot that been marked for her many years ago at the edge of our mesa remained empty.

• • •

A second trip interrupted the winter idyll by the ocean on Aquidneck Island. Traveling briefly to San Francisco on my birthday, I arrived late and woke the next morning to see the sun rise while a crescent moon still hung in the sky. Layers of orange, russet cream, pale blue, indigo, and blue black filled the horizon. The calm gave way to loss, again to thoughts of Halflife. I wanted to laugh and saw only decay.

I had returned to San Francisco to visit Anna who had started her treatments for cancer. She had called me and asked me to visit while her husband was away. Before our rendezvous, I walked by my old haunts, including Mario's Bohemian Cigar Store, my former corner cafe. Gone were its proprietors from Trieste: the old man with square skull and irritable disposition and his lanky gap-toothed, good natured wife. Gone, their son, a big-shoul-dered brute with a mustache. Gone, all the other characters of the neighborhood, none of whom could afford to live there anymore. Bypassing the café, I wandered the rainy streets in my former neighborhood, mourning a community that had once been there. San Francisco, such a beautiful lady, was a city of death.

When Anna and I met in a park at Union Square, we talked about grief and anger. The words cannot be conjured now, but we talked about resolving one's self before death as the obligation at hand, and maybe that some comfort could be found in the resolution. We talked and walked towards the piers that once had cargo ships, and she cried in my arms, saying *There is so much to live for. There is so much to live for.* She sobbed, and as I held her, I felt her heart beating in her cancerous chest and, after a few moments, some release, a letting go.

After two days I left Anna, and she appeared in good spirits. She had decided to follow a regimen of herbal teas to stem her cancer. An herbalist in Chinatown as-sembled the herbs, which she boiled at home for her cure. But shortly after I returned to the island, she called and left a message saying that she was struggling with her cancer more than before. When I called her back, she told me about a dream in which in a room of a large complex house she met a young radiant girl with whom she fell deeply in love. In another room she saw five disgusting men, cavemen and Vikings. Barbaric and brutal, they were beating each other with two-by-fours, and one was sniffing the genitals of another. In a third scene she entered a room filled with books where a retainer, a young man, was cleaning. She told the young man she had to pass through the room, and he replied that was impossible. She insisted until he relented and moved aside a group of books to reveal a two-foot square hole. Anna climbed through the opening to the next room where she saw both the glowing girl and the hairy barbarians, but none saw the other. The girl was safe for the moment. And then Anna awoke.

• • •

Insomnia hit me two nights running in the late darkness of winter on the island. Perhaps the quiet of the middle night draws a light sleeper to waking in order to process thoughts and the inner world when all else is still. In the old days, spring brought sleepless nights. Moonlight on clouds woke me often. Only the rarest images remained of my ex-wife, but I often imagined holding and caressing Anna. I knew I would visit her again, but I grew afraid. If we kissed and our tongues exchanged saliva, would the cancer cells pass to me? If my seed entered her, would my sex absorb the poison that runs through her? Would she tell me if she has AIDS?

• • •

I had to leave the island refuge a third time to travel to New York. On the train from Providence a woman sitting opposite me told her story. She was an actress going to the city for the opening of a film in which she had a small part as a school teacher on whom her teenage students played tricks. The actress had been in the country on tragic family business. Her mother, who managed real estate, had been murdered one night in an office in one of the buildings she owned. According to the actress, three of the tenants murdered her because the woman had sent one of them an eviction notice. The tenants still lived in the building, unapprehended, and the daughter had gone up to settle the estate and help in the police investigation.

During our conversation the actress told me her name and where she lived. Toward the end of the journey to the city I looked up to see her staring at the ceiling, tears pouring from her eyes. There was no sobbing, but pain filled her face. No one else saw the tears, and when the train arrived at the station, I turned to her on the platform and said, *your grief will pass*. Her tears returned instantly and she said, *If only my mother could come to the opening of the film*. *She knows*, I replied. *She knows*. But as I walked away I doubted my own convictions in what the dead know of the living.

• • •

I had gone to New York in response to a call from my lawyer who informed me that my Uncle Bill had died, not recently but one month earlier. The fact that he had died, that he been in a nursing home, that he was even close to death was shocking. I was amazed that I had found out so late. I was the one charged with trying to prepare him for the days when his various ailments would incapacitate him. I was the one whom he called usually on a Saturday night to tell his rambling stories, which often were repeated when he called back a few minutes later simply to continue the conversation as if we had never said good-bye. Long silences followed those calls. I occasionally called him, but as he had decided no one ever called him, he would not answer the phone. When an unscrupulous, distant cousin tried to badger him into making the cousin his sole heir, I brought Uncle Bill to a lawyer so he could make his own will. I did try to arrange for him to get a nurse or to have an emergency alert system, but he refused both. I wrote him, but not often enough. Sometimes I imagined that he would die alone in his apartment and be discovered weeks later, an odiferous corpse.

Now his perplexed nephew had discovered his death weeks after it occurred, but the state of his bent body remained unknown. A scoliotic retired clerk, he lived alone, occasionally heard voices, and wore rumpled and stained suits. The paranoia that he sometimes exhibited by saying that a giant machine monitored his calls through the walls of his flat, and his peculiar obsessions – one week with vitamins, another week with a computer disk he received in the mail – did not prevent him from utter lucidity about events in the news or accounts of family activities that he cobbled together.

Still I wondered where was his body? In a pauper's grave, like a ward of the state? In a funeral home morgue? On ice somewhere? In a pile of ash? Although he may have appeared to be a pauper, he was not, and he did have some family, even if only a distant nephew and pair of nieces. I can only assume that he forgot or did not have the cogency to tell someone the name of his next of kin. We had plans for his burial: he was to be interred on Aquidneck Island in the family plot by the side of the aunt and uncle who had raised him and my father. A religious ceremony and proper burial were planned. My father had died without me by his side, and I hoped I might do better by his brother. In the end strangers carted him off to a nursing home, somewhere, and strangers saw his last days. I had thought he should have some dignity and a little of the family he never enjoyed as he lay dying.

I wondered what happened to his apartment. Uncle Bill had lived in the small apartment with my grandfather and his wife until they divorced. When grandfather died, the uncle stayed on another thirty years in rent-controlled security. The apartment changed little while the neighborhood morphed from a small Jewish neighborhood to a small Black neighborhood. The place he lived had been off limits to me – we always met elsewhere – and I was secretly glad because I feared its disarray, piles, smell, the oldness of it all. Eventually, I would need to visit and close the apartment. Would I find unopened bills, worthless stock certificates, stained clothes, his weird artifacts, huge stacks of the Harvard Health Magazines, laundry hung to dry, and somewhere the few relics of family history that had been my great grandfather's: a prayer book, silver menorah, and wine decanter? Or would I discover that all his possessions had been carted to the incinerator or distributed among his neighbors and that a new family occupied the flat of the strange, bent man?

Uncle Bill's death remained mysterious as I discovered that someone had claimed his body and buried him, but I did not know who. Dealing with the morgue and court by phone was difficult. Nobody wanted to be helpful, except for a nice clerk at the post office who said she would hold Uncle Bill's mail for ten days. I left New York, knowing I would need to return before his affairs would be settled.

• • •

I returned to Aquidneck Island and soon saw the beginnings of spring as the young corn emerged in rows of green on the local farms. When I wandered again along the beach, enjoying the changing angle of light, I reflected on the transience of intimacy. People whom you feel are close friends disappear from your life. People who spend years of their lives together, making love, sharing the most intimate details, tasting each others vital fluids, separate, rupture, and become total strangers, one not even recognizing the other. Your heart pounds for someone, and when you hold them in your arms, you feel and honestly believe that the shared intimacy is permanent. Then one day, years later, you see her at a museum and can't remember her name. Oh, yes, ups and downs, but intimacy will last. Why shouldn't it? But it does not last. All those ex-spouses with whom, beyond sex, we share children, property, growth, pain, laughter, and boredom split apart, and that person becomes like every other stranger, and you ask yourself, I spent my life with him? I did that with her? We joined to make children? And the one you count on most, the one you found after all the others left you (or whom you left), that one will leave you too, and you will forget the taste of her mouth and rhythm of her pulse.

No body, no thing stays close. All fall away. And you get the message that intimacy is inappropriate for this time and age, a romantic idea, spent long ago. Wanting intimacy, and certainly wanting it sustained, is a mark of weakness, a sign of somebody out of step with the program. But is this accurate? Is the absence of intimacy more now than it ever was?

I wanted to submerge myself in some new work. Once submerged, feelings of loneliness would disappear, and self and the world would meld. *Submerge into a chrysalis,* I told myself. *By late spring, you will be a different creature, a secret shape-shifter not by choice, but by circumstance, by life. If I had the magic I should have, I would leave loss behind and join Leonard Cohen, the great roué, for his last tour.*

• • •

The time of refuge in the island cottage came to a close, and I prepared to leave my ancestors' turf. The departure was as lonely as any day during this temporary sojourn. Boxes were packed, the house arranged, and quiet filled the rooms, as I waited for morning light to depart. I thought of Anna and composed some words for her that remained unsent: *My thoughts are with you now. Your image remains clear. Wherever you are I send you my care and love.*

Returning to my house in Texas, I stopped to conclude arranging my Uncle's affairs in New York. Having received all the official permissions, I was finally able to gain access to Uncle Bill's apartment, which had been unoccupied for six months. Instead of a place of human habitation, I found a rat's nest, a dystopia violently ransacked after my uncle's death. His stepmother's paintings still hung on the walls. Her books were still on the shelves, but the typescripts which had been carefully filed were scattered into the flotsam of trash like dried roses tossed by a thunderstorm. The debris and trash were layered piles to a uniform depth of ten inches, except where drawers and cupboards had been dumped into mounds. Decades of dust covered whatever was not upturned. The violence of whoever ransacked the place filled the air. The whole history of our family had ended up in a pile of filth and rubbish. Anything of material value – if there had been anything at all – had been stolen. I returned to Villa Trice with whatever I could load into two suitcases, including a patch from the World's Fair of 1939, which was miraculously pristine.

MEMPHIS

Henry's crypt lay high up on the side of a large octagonal columbarium. A tall ladder or scaffolding was needed to pull out the stone plaque and lay his ashes within. Next to his crypt already lay the place of his partner, William, who remained alive and grieving. The lower rows of stones held the names of some well known Memphians. Fluorescent lights, hidden in coved moldings, overlit the interior adding a coldness. The building, an octagon in the center of a picturesque cemetery, made no sense.

Only a few hours earlier I had spoken at the public memorial held at the art school to which Henry had devoted much of his life. Having just retired and full of plans, Henry had been walking down his driveway, stooped to pick up his cat, fell over, crashed onto his face, and in turning and hitting the ground, broke his hip. His hospital stay had been longer than expected, and he was kept horizontal in traction for many days until the bones mended adequately for his return home. Coming home, he appeared to continue to convalesce, but one morning after sitting up at breakfast, he keeled over, gasping for air, and died. The doctors at the hospital had neglected to give him a blood thinner, a normal precaution, and his inactivity in bed had caused a clot to form in his leg. The clot traveled that morning to his heart, and suddenly Henry was gone. Halflife exceeded, the full turning of his life had ended at age sixty-five.

The news of his death had been shattering for me. Having reconnected to him after an absence of years, I looked forward to caring for him as I would have for my own father. In the days I spent in Memphis before his funeral and afterwards, many memories returned to me of the life I had lived there.

• • •

My birth certificate says that I was born on Camilla Street where my parents and older sister lived in an apartment. I had no recollection of Camilla Street. Among the few photographs I had of our family, one showed me in a stroller wearing a diaper with my thumb stuck out as if I was hitching a ride with a huge smile on my face, a delirious grin of infinite pleasure. Another photograph showed me as a baby with my older sister having a birthday party. The event appeared splendid even though my sister was gangly and unattractive. (Truly a late bloomer, she later became one of the great southern belles of town.) The little birthday party was mixed with black and white children all looking finely dressed. Where they came from, I have no idea, perhaps the offspring of a maid who helped my mother. My sister craned over a birthday present as everyone looked around with glee, and in the background was that funny place on Camilla Street. Down the road lived a young Greek couple, Nick and Hazel, who became great friends of my parents. Nick operated a junk yard off Main Street. My father was very fond of him, and when I was older, my father took me to visit Nick at the junk yard located behind a leaning wooden wall erected to hide the marvels of junk held within. I could sense that Hazel, his wife, loved me. Since they had no children of their own, she would watch with delight as I ran run up and down the halls of their house when we visited them. I raced like a madman on all fours as everyone roared with laughter. But Camilla Street was only a picture and some stories.

The other memories of childhood come from the house at 717 White Station Road. The street was a quiet lane that marked the city limits. With no sidewalks it was just a rough edge of asphalt at the city's edge. That first house I remembered as a child was far too small for a family of five—my parents, my older sister and the younger one who soon arrived, and myself – but its smallness allowed me to eavesdrop on the rare parties that my parents had. My younger sister and I would be tucked into bed, pretending to sleep, but in fact I was listening to my mother playing the piano in the room next to us and to people laughing, drinking, and enjoying themselves. I loved listening to the grownups' social activities. When my parents went out to parties, which was infrequent, I waited up for them to come back. The window, parallel to my bed, was a secret portal to the outer world at night, and I would sit up, prop my chin on its sill, look out, and wait for the sound of the old Chevrolet coming up our short, steep driveway. That window also allowed a means of daring escape from the obligation of being in bed at some certain hour. Once in this gazing mode I noticed snow crystals had started to fall. The event was so rare that, thrilled, I woke up Denise, my younger sister. Clad in pajamas, I convinced her to climb out the window with me. We snaked along the narrow brick ledge, dropped down into the hedge, and then ran into the snow as it fell. After an inch had accumulated, I lay down and made a snow angel, an intuitive gesture lodged innately in the psyche of all little beings. Those crystals intoxicated us in the middle of the night; the frost intrigued our fingers.

We played an exhilarating game in this small house on White Station Road. A large attic fan, situated in the ceiling of the hall, had metal shutters that could be opened and started by the pull of a chain with a plastic knob at its end. Once opened, the immense fan situated above the louvers sucked air up at a voracious rate into the attic which might have well have been the greatest void ever known. Standing under this great sucking monster you could feel the air swirl around you as it licked off the bits of sweat that had collected in the summer heat. The cooling effect was only a minor pleasure compared to the experience of taking sheets of white notebook paper, the kind with thin blue lines and three holes on the side, wadding those sheets up as tight as possible, and gently tossing them up to watch the sucking mouth devour them one after another. I must have sent a thousand wads of paper into the attic, but it never seemed filled.

As a small child Jiminy Cricket became my favorite Disney cartoon character – his weird body was spell binding and his admonition, "Let your conscience be your guide," appeared then as the sagest advice. Jiminy Cricket spoke from a little TV and from records played at the speed of 78 revolutions per minute. We had a strange contraption for playing those 78 rpms: an old RCA record player. Housed in a wooden case with foldout top, it had a crooked, thin center spindle on which the records were placed. The speed of the record was selected, a lever flicked, and the crook allowed a little clevis to hold them in place until the mechanism dropped them ferociously to the turn table. A thin swinging arm kept the records steady while perched on the spindle. When the record landed, it spun fast, and all you wanted to do was run your fingers over the record to slow it down. Conversely, you could slow a 33 rpm down even further to 16½ rpm, which sounded so droll, like someone on drugs, but you had no idea of drugs then. There was also an attachment—a stubby, plastic phallic cylinder – you could place over the skinny spindle, which would allow you to stack up 45's. So ingenious was this machine that the clevis also operated the adapter, sending two metal disks to drop a record while keeping the stack in place. There was another boxy machine for 45's only, something that looked like a make-up case when closed, but Ruth, my older sister, horded it for herself. That was the least of what she deserved. A mysterious and lonely outsider, she had already been exiled by my parents to an emotional Siberia, for reasons that were unclear to me.

Jiminy Cricket joined characters from the *Wind and the Willows*, all of whom I wanted to be my most special and best friends, particularly Toad of Toad Hall. Should they decide to visit me, they were all welcomed in Elf Land, a domain that comprised the front yard on the house on White Station Road. It was my first place of refuge. To my eyes the front yard had hills, though really nubs, and roots and ravines covered in honey suckle; it was the magic place of childhood, a place for watching the clouds and looking for eagles to return to the nest in the gnarly tree.

• • •

The history of the street name was lost. No one ever talked about White Station as a place, or whoever White was. At the corner of the road, intersecting the major thoroughfare of Poplar Avenue, was Mr. Pope's house, a tumbling wreck surrounded by screened porches. Always dressed in overalls, Mr. Pope was a yard man. Across Poplar Avenue lay the Tropical Freeze, a drive-in ice cream shop, run by a mother and son; it was one of my favorite destinations. Heading down White Station Road, in the opposite direction after Mr. Pope's house were our neighbors: Sweetie Smith, who grew strawberries; the non-descript couple whose daughter Bonnie had bucked teeth; our house; then below our house, Mrs. Brooks, a widower who had no almost no furniture in her house; Dick and Beverly Downing, a couple who had no children but, amazingly, kept a slot machine in a closet; and Jack and Connie Garver, whose daughter Betty Lee was one of my closest friends. The topography of the road rose at that point and on the raised land were Mr. and Mrs. Earl Hooker, Jr., both of whom had thick Mississippi accents and drove Cadillacs; and the Jacques, a nice family of strangers from some distant place, maybe as far as Canada, and whose name we pronounced Jakeweeze. At the end of the residences lay a small raw Baptist church of white clapboard.

Beyond the church was a derelict farm. Sometimes I explored this place alone or at times with a friend. Who he was I cannot remember, maybe Wesley Summers or Rusty Turner. Or maybe this was a friend I invented as I always felt a dearth of male companionship.

The place must have been originally a farm located very far from the city, a miniscule plantation with small acreage though trees covering the site obscured its full extent. Turning from the road over a rough timber structure with a big culvert bridging our creek (in truth a ragged drainage ditch), a dirt drive, honed by tire tracks, formed two depressions with a grassy hump between them. To the right of the drive were fields that seemed barely tended as bramble bushes grew at their edges.

The drive dipped then ascended to a wooden house of two stories, board and batten in construction with a long porch on its front. Though it appeared empty, we could never be certain it was abandoned. Behind the house on the west the hill sloped down as the drive curved slowly northward to end at a dilapidated group of farm buildings and sheds.

The hill provided a vista of other uncultivated fields, long filled with berry bushes, sassafras, and trees that made a rough green mat. Far to the west was a field planted in cotton or corn where I once saw a man with a mule plowing the earth. Beside that field was a small creek, the site of many of my mud dams, twig forts, and the location of an old leather holster that I assumed must have been a Civil War relic.

I knew even as a seven-year-old boy that the place was eccentric, an odd glimmer of rural life at the edge of the largest city in the state. To me it was enchanted, and my favorite forays focused on the barn and the round pond beyond it. Located north of the house, the barn was locked but had ragged boards with eyelets for peaking within. The floor was soft earth, still moist, and the whole place smelled of manure, corn cobs, and whiskers of straw. Blackberry bushes completely surrounded the barn and provided not only succulent fruit but superb cover from whoever might see me prowling about the premises. The bushes rose six to eight feet, up to the eaves of the barn's roof and wrapped around it. Trying to avoid being seen, I crawled around the bottoms of the bushes, searching for a branch that would inflict the fewest cuts as I climbed upward and finally heaved myself onto the steeply sloping metal, glistening in the sun. The corrugated metal could be burning hot during the big heat when tar would ooze from the seams and could be pulled up and rolled into small spheres that resembled gooey black marbles. Along with the exhilaration of the view came the fear of falling off the roof into my own briar patch like Bre'er Rabbit, impaled by the thorns.

The roof allowed splendid views of the whole terrain, and on the hipped west side, sheltered from prying eyes of the house, I could observe the pond from on high. A perfect circle, the pond was mocha in color even when its edges shrank in the dry times to leave a slick continuous band of glistening mud resembling a monk's tonsure. Dragon flies skimmed over the surface, slapping their abdomens onto the water as the females deposited eggs, and at night animals would come to drink. I steered clear of ever entering the pond. The mud sides look more slippery than my mother's bathtub in which I sloshed back and forth in a sea of Nivea oil, the most efficient lubricant I knew at that time. If I ever fell into the green slime, I doubted I would emerge.

I visited the farm often, exploring the barn, the thickets and fields, and stream whose source, if followed completely, would lead to the Mississippi River itself. On numerous occasions I planned to pursue it to the source, and realized the trip would require several days. Slowly I assembled the necessary supplies and equipment from an army surplus store—canteen, hatchet, canvas belt with grommets, matches—but the trip never took place.

Eventually the land was sold to make a swim club, a complex advertised as the most advanced aquatic center in the city. When I could get free, I would head down White Station Road and survey the construction under way. In no time heavy equipment had stripped every blackberry bush and leveled every knoll. The house disappeared, but the construction suddenly stopped as the site turned into a muddy marsh while the land took its revenge. Huge concrete culverts were brought in to redirect the flow of the heavy rains, but the land's protest was brief. Eventually, the swim club with its two Olympic size pools and diving pit and an adjacent slender brick locker room, emerged. The swimmers who practiced there, members of the MAC (Memphis Athletic Club), were the fiercest and best competitors in the city. I once swam against one of them in a state meet. Poorly trained (Mr. Fulghum, a military retiree who took care of the country club pool did not push us hard in training), I was no match for the MAC swimmer, and I came in third place, an experience as terrifying as it was humiliating.

• • •

During my adolescence Memphis became for me a musky, sensual, and occasionally tragic place. There were many stories of struggle and even death that may have paralleled the lives of teenagers elsewhere, but I have no way of knowing. One friend in junior high school, Gene J., was very strange. He had double jointed fingers which he often cracked, and we often snuck out in cars at night to cruise the city until dawn. Once, we took his older sister's car, and were stopped by the police. On another occasion he told me that in his attic he had a cage in which he tortured squirrels that he caught. His face contorted in laughter as he recounted this to me, enjoying my horror. He fell in love with a beautiful blond haired boy, who attended another school in the center of town. Increasingly, the two of them retreated, excluding me from their friendship. On arriving at school one day, I was told they had entered into a suicide pact and killed themselves on the previous evening. Shotguns to the head.

I had another friend, Richard S., who resembled a little James Dean. Presenting himself to the world as a rebel, he laughed with a sweetness that James Dean never knew. He had his hair trimmed in a crew cut, not because he was so straight like the red necks from whom he descended, but as a comment on the greasers of the 1950s. Mocking and laughing at everything around him, including his sassy self, he was full of life. He rolled the sleeves of his tee shirts up to his shoulders, and when there were no adults around to catch him, he folded in a pack of cigarettes too. But he did get caught, and he talked backed to his parents not to attack them, but to counter their charges. The beatings his father inflicted with a tooled leather belt never broke his spirit. We heard Richard S. wail during his whipping, but he would be laughing afterwards and still sneak out later that night, because sneaking out and borrowing a car were our entries to a world beyond parental control. His father installed sheet metal ducts, and his mother had those sweet bitch looks that make men in taverns late at night loose control. They came from the country, maybe Sardis, Tunica Cutoff, Bolivar, or Greenville, someplace in Mississippi where sharecropping had died and cotton no longer supported anyone.

My first girlfriend, Sarah A., had rural southern roots, but her father was a Cherokee born on the reservation in Oklahoma. Small and quiet, he ran a beer joint on the south side of town and hunted deer during the season. He always frightened me, and when we saw each other we never spoke. Her mother was friendly and warm; she had large rings around her eyes from chain smoking and endless coffee which she drank to stay up at night until her husband came home from the bar. My girlfriend's older sister, Lucy, was part of Elvis Presley's entourage; their families were actually related by blood. Sometimes Elvis would send a car for the sister—she would leave all dressed up fifties style with tall hair to visit Graceland. It all seemed so natural. The sister was lovely and sweet in a gentle southern way. She made a living selling aluminum siding. She would drive through the countryside in a big Cadillac, her skirt hiked up to tan her legs, until she found some ramshackle house where she stopped and extolled the benefits of metal siding.

My first girlfriend was unusual in every respect. To me she was quite beautiful, but difficult to describe. Her nose was upturned, her eyes sparkled green, her brunette hair framed a delicate face, and her lips were full. She had a scent too, something like corn, that I assume emanated from her perfume. I loved her and gave her a ring to confirm that we were going steady. She had stopped going to public school in the seventh grade; the strain of it was too much for her. Her parents hired a tutor to continue her education, a training that was interrupted by occasional visits to Indian relatives in Oklahoma. In addition to school being an unbearable burden, the fear of rejection terrified her.

I walked to her house every day after school and spent two hours kissing on the sofa in her living room. While we kissed and held each other and rocked in passion, her mother sat on the other side of the wall, smoking in the kitchen and drinking coffee. Usually, after two hours I called my mother to come pick me up, which she did grudgingly as she harshly disapproved of my girlfriend. My mother was still well enough to drive.

Once, I thought I had accidentally killed my first girl-friend. We were lying on the sofa, kissing and pressing against each other undulating, grinding, pubis against pubis, searching through our clothes for the union both desired but did not understand. We called it hunching. Some people called it dry fucking. The rhythm of kissing and hunching increased in lurches so strong that we gasped for breath. Her breathing quickened, her eyes rolled back into her until only the whites shown. Suddenly, she gasped and quivered from foot to head, and then lay still and motionless. The lack of movement frightened me. *Are you alright*, I asked repeatedly as she lay listless. Then I shivered as I feared that she had had a heart attack—I had accidentally hunched her to death. I slapped her face to revive her. No movement. And panic soared as I thought about her mother sitting on the other side of the wall, waiting for her husband who would first beat the hell out of me and then shoot me like a dumb deer. I began to rehearse what I would say to her mother: *Oh Mrs. A, I am terribly sorry, but Sarah and I were hunching and she had a heart attack, so could you please call an ambulance.* This plea proved unnecessary. Sarah slowly wakened, looked at me quizzically, and had no explanation of what happened in the first rocking orgasm of her life.

This intense physicality mirrored her feelings. Another event proved more life threatening. Although I had no words for it, I sometimes experienced her emotional need as overwhelming. The sensation was a fear, a responsibility I had for her because I loved her. Being thirteen years old, the feeling was frightening. In an attempt to get some emotional distance from her, I asked her to return the initial ring I gave her to indicate we were going steady. Over the phone she cried. Then, she locked herself in her bedroom and slit her wrists with a razor blade. Her mother found her under circumstances I have never known, and took her to the emergency room where they bandaged her wrists. When I saw her wrists circled in gauze, I knew I would never ask for the ring again. This slitting happened more than once; she never returned to school, and I never saw her after I was sent away to boarding school.

I had no fear then about opening my heart to another, and ever since that encounter I have tried to open my self as the primal act of loving another. It was not always easy, but when I was able, I felt as if my highest and best self emerged. By comparison, everything else was simply an aspect of the job at hand. The opening hearts with others continued to move me.

• • •

Thinking of Henry as a pile of ashes heaved up high into the octagon made me also think of mother. Some memories remained of my mother operating intact in the world. When my younger sister followed me across Poplar Avenue to get an ice cream and a pick up truck hit her, my mother acted with surprising rationality as she dressed and rushed to the ambulance. Without panic she moved more efficiently and calmly than I had ever seen; terrified and guilty, I was relieved to discover my sister suffered only a broken collar bone. When my mother found old Mrs. Brooks dead, fully dressed on of the floor of her empty parlor, she acted with similar calm. I remember how she worked to shelter Hungarian refugees in the revolt of 1956. And once my mother told me about labor unions and what it meant to never cross a picket line; I was no older than twelve. But mostly I remember her face in agony, her moans, her screams. I remember our fights until the time she said I was the only reason she was staying alive, and from that point forward I no longer raised my voice. Her cancer knew no Halflife and its mutating cells overwhelmed their neighbor cells with grim speed. How does cancer pick its victims? Does it accept recommendations? Is cancer's face the image of goat-headed death?

My mother's continued illness and the pallor it laid over our family led to my being sent to boarding school away from girl friends and crazy mates who tortured squirrels. My older sister, though barely nineteen, had been instrumental in finding a good school for me. When I left the fecund south, the only home I had known, for chilly New England, I missed my fragmented family and the life of art that had begun forming inside me.

• • •

Prior to my discovery of romantic love, my parents had sent me at the age of twelve to the art academy in Overton Park where I studied pottery and ceramics. Thorne Edwards, a tall Nordic figure with a perfectly trimmed gray beard, taught the ceramics class for young people. I spent all Saturday mornings trying to center wet clay on the plaster bat atop a rotating wheel, and increasingly I stayed on into the afternoons to watch Mr. Edwards and his regular students load the great kilns. To judge temperatures they inserted triangular wedges of clay that would warp successively as the temperate increased. The warping process could be observed through a small bung hole: inside the kiln everything glowed fiery orange, even the air itself, and to the side one could see the cones slowly warping. After the long cycles of heating and cooling and the kilns were emptied, I examined these curved cones as much as the bowls, pots and objects that emerged from this immense inferno.

I spent many days in the studio, but I never mastered the wheel. Perhaps my hands were too small and the necessary coordination lacking, however, I felt more in control of making mosaics. A special pair of pliers with sharp flared ends allowed snipping the colored tiles to fill patterns that had been drawn onto squares of plywood a quarter of an inch think. The tiles were blues and greens, grays and beiges, and an occasional brilliant gold. The images came out of my head as some kind of imagery landscape. Perhaps even then visions of Elf Land were inspiring me. After cutting and attaching the tiles, Mr. Edwards showed how to mix the grout that would be smeared about the tile and into the slots and grooves around their edges. A burlap cloth rubbed over the surface removed the excess grout and repeated rubbings provided a sheen. Later, I realized this filling and rubbing process applied to inking etched and engraved plates.

Often as I fumbled at the wheel on those quiet afternoons the adult students would come to work. All of them moved silently, and I watched in amazement as Fred Bauer, gaunt with a light red goatee, raised thin towers of porcelain as his long arms plunged into a mound of clay while his fingers defined the thinnest of walls. These cylinders and turrets would be mounted one upon another to create totems which would be fired and glazed in exquisite earth tones. Bauer never spoke to me, and I dared not interfere with his concentration. He also made glazed reliquaries for the ashes of the dead. He was a Buddhist, a fact that seemed very strange to me in the context of a conservative southern town, and these cinerary urns somehow figured into the rituals of Buddhism. Or at least that is what I imagined from the shadows of the pottery studio.

The pottery studio connected to the sculpture studio, a vast room with a high ceiling that dripped with amorphous plaster shapes. White sculptures in various states, ranging from thin, plaster soaked sheets over chicken wire and steel armatures to abstract figures with rasped surfaces, stood freely on their own or sat on tripods. Gossamer fabrics floated in front of the large windows and plaster dust coated every surface. Amidst this frosted environment John McIntire presided. Tall and gaunt, his scraggly goatee accentuated his narrow angular face from which warm and impish smiles constantly poured. Unlike Mr. Edwards who was somber and serious, Mr. McIntire had the spirit of sprite, a refugee from a *Midsummer Night's Dream*. I loved wandering through the sculpture studio, marveling at the spatulas and rasps and rifflers—all tools for working plaster—as well as the corner set aside for welding metal, but I never took a class in the sculpture studio.

The two studios opened onto a courtyard. Rectangular in plan, it combined a series of stone parterres, benches, gardens and ponds to resemble a space that was Japanese in spirit and sensibility; Memphis was very Japanese. Modules of squares organized everything, and the courtyard provided not only a pleasant space to move through but a visual focus for the main studios around it. As the studios were twenty feet high, they flanked the courtyard so it remained hidden to the eyes of outsiders. Beyond the courtyard on the north was a wide corridor leading to steel doors painted gray that opened onto a path to the street.

At the opposite end beyond the courtyard sat a small cafeteria, operated by a blind man named Hubert. I must have seen blind people before my first glimpse of Hubert, but I never had the chance to interact with them or observe them at length. Thin, like a sheaf of dried grass, his angular face with sharp nose resembled the face of a possum. Tinted glasses covered the sockets for what had been eyes and a purplish flesh emanating around these slits contrasted with the flat white of his skin. He sometimes wore a baggy sports coat, sometimes polyester shirts with ribbed fronts. He usually stayed behind the counter from which he served hot and cold sandwiches and drinks. To heat the sandwiches Hubert put them into a box with coils to warm up the bread and melt the cheese. I found these sandwiches with thin sliced meats delicious, and I would order them though I always felt slightly guilty as Hubert went through the relentless ritual of trying to retrieve the correct sandwich and feel his way to the hot box. After downing a sandwich I often ate an ice cream confection, usually a Nutty Buddy, which consisted of a waffle cone with vanilla ice cream wrapped in chocolate and ground nuts. Often I would be the only person eating in the cafeteria in late afternoon—lunch was the busiest time—and I would watch Hubert who ran a pile of coins through his fingers the way that poker players run chips through theirs. I could tell he was always intensely listening for anyone approaching his counter, and I wondered if he perceived a young boy at the far table. His day at work ended as it began, when someone came to lead him from behind the counter to the rear door where a car was waiting.

A painting studio and the weaving and textile studio lay across the courtyard. After pottery I began studying painting with Martha Turner. A small woman with gray hair and large glasses, she had long fingers whose joints were already gnarly, a sign of the arthritis that would eventually cripple her. But in those days she demonstrated the wonders of tempera paints, and taught us how to make dynamic compositions from the still lifes she set up for us in her studio. Most importantly, she communicated the life of color in everything we painted. No overt theory was needed as we could see with our eyes how brilliant colors came to life—blues, greens, magentas, sunny yellows. And she showed us that brushes were only tools and when needed, the tips of our fingers laid in color or made marks that defied any brush stroke.

The weaving and textile studio, next to Martha's studio, soon became my second home. The studio was filled with floor looms, mostly made by Macomber and Leclerq, and a spinning wheel and long table were located in one corner. Henry started me on a small metal loom that sat on a table. The little loom was wide enough to learn double weave, a technique that produced a tube which you could use to make a pillow or cushion. Eventually I moved to larger looms. Henry taught me to wind the warp on the back beam of a loom. The strands of yarn would be brought forward and threaded one by one through the eyes in the vertical metal holders called heddles, and secured to the front beam. The heddles were secured in frames called harnesses, and the raising and lowering of the harnesses in sequence provided the openings in the warp that allowed the weaver to pass yarn across the warp at right angles. Some kinds of special threading sequences through the heddles allowed for intricate patterns when you followed a series of directions for raising and lowering the harnesses. Henry taught me the traditional patterns of Whig Rose and Lover's Knot which relied on this kind of system. He also taught me rug techniques that required learning to tie the basic kinds of knots, Turkish Ghiordes and Persian Senneh. The lengths of the rug tufts had Scandinavian names, flossa for the long ones, and rya for the short ones. Henry introduced me to myriads of yarns from the finest wools of Paternayen yarns, intensely saturated with Procion dyes, to a whole array of linens, and even metallic yarns.

Although there was no snobbery about technique or media, it became clear that the acme of the art was found in tapestry. Henry taught me the challenging methods of Gobelin and Aubusson factories of ancient France. From those days on I studied their techniques of the interlacing of one thread over another, the building up of gradients of color that lay at the center of creating a three-dimensional pictorial illusionism, and eventually I saw great wall hangings at the Louvre, and the Unicorns at the Cloisters in New York. The history of art was always of interest, but we saw ourselves as modernists, artists who abstracted the world around them.

• • •

My parents appeared to support the life of the young artist in their midst. With no trepidation they left me in Henry's hands, to spend hours studying with him or visiting his stone cottage or spending time with the other artists around him. No threat existed in the eccentric behavior of a small demi-monde, refugees who found at the academy not only their voices, but their freedoms. No fear attended Henry's homosexuality. We all existed among tacit understandings. I never knew how far my mother's support would extend to my life as an artist; she died in the middle of my freshman year at college, delirious, and finally freed from an agony of long duration. My father eventually made his view clear on the insecure life an artist would lead, expressing finally the fear that had run his own life from the very day his own mother died when he, like me, was in his eighteenth year, the very half of Halflife itself.

• • •

After Henry's memorial I returned to the villa in Texas that remained my home, but a dull grief hung over me. The activities of teaching and writing books about architecture resumed. The cycle of soft winter and early spring continued. The pond in the front yard came to life, the wisteria poured over the side terrace. But other events intervened.

Anna, whose image had remained with me all those years, called to say that she was going to the hospital for tests about the state of her cancer. She hoped her regime had put the disease into remission. She sounded strong, but her voice quivered. She mentioned that when she had gone for her herbs, the herbalist was absent, *passed away*, his old Chinese wife said cryptically. Anna told me of another of her dreams in which she received a letter from me that literally glowed. The letter took the form of a pictogram of magic words and images and a Michelangelesque drawing of a female nude. Later, she called to say that the cancer in her lungs was not growing, but the cancer in her liver had doubled in size. She asked me if I would return to visit her while her husband was away on business. The prognosis was unclear, but she decided to try more aggressive chemotherapy, and, if it failed, other alternative medicines.

I sat on the plane replaying our conversation. Part of me was terrified. No Halflife limits cancer cells as they overwhelm tissues and organs in their mutagenic dance of growth gone mad. Upon arrival I called Anna who told me she could not speak at length, that she had declined steeply, and that she had hospice care. I could feel her dying even at that distance. When I finally saw her, I saw a different body with changed skin color and a swollen stomach. In the evening I held her close to me and felt her sweating. As I entered her I could not distinguish rapture from her pain. Did I touch the last place of Eros in her, or did I shove myself against the distended walls of her cancerous organs? The sound of her moan has never left me.

A few days after I left Anna, she fell out of bed during the night. Unable to move, she groaned on the floor until morning when her nurse found her. Confusion among Emergency Medical Services sent her from one hospital to the next. Her husband blundered ineffectually in not getting her quickly to her doctor. She died a day after entering the hospital. Her husband had her body cremated and her ashes scattered over San Francisco Bay.

• • •

Within the year I had married for the second time. Patricia and I united in our shared status of being orphans. Laughing and bickering, sharing much but temperamentally different, we nurtured each other as best we could. Not long after we settled into Villa Trice, a letter arrived from Memphis that cryptically announced a private sale of the entire contents of the estate of Henry and William, his companion. I wondered why William would be selling everything they owned. Perhaps he was moving to a smaller residence. The sale was only four days ahead so I called him, but the phone rang without answer. When I called the organizers of the sale, I was told William had died three months before. Shocked, I searched for his obituary, which said he had died of natural causes and named the heirs who presumably were selling the property. I could not leave on such short notice, and Patricia volunteered to travel to Memphis and buy something of Henry's privately before the public sale of his estate.

All arrangements were rushed, but she arrived early the morning of the sale. Inside were the artifacts of two life times of collecting and making: wall hangings, drawings, fabrics, paintings, photographs, furniture, African figural sculptures, obelisks of various sizes, boxes of all sizes and materials. Patricia bought one of Henry's recent, large wall hangings of bamboo wrapped in silk, two gouache studies, two early collages, a figural drawing by Ted Rust, the former director of the art school, a small pencil drawing by Thorne Edwards, a collage by William, and a photograph by one of Henry's friends. When she called to tell me about the purchases, she started crying as she said *It is all so sad*, which it was, and I too began crying. She said she also had something very special to give me that Henry had always wanted me to have. Patricia discovered that William had not died of natural causes: as he had threatened during the time of Henry's funeral, he had drunk himself to death. Veda, Henry's closest friend and neighbor, later told me Bill had become a recluse and would not even see her. She found him dead in a pool of blood on Thanksgiving day.

When Patricia returned to the villa, she brought many of the art works with her, but not the big wall hanging which was too delicate to ship. I made a small impromptu exhibition of this little memorial hoard, and then Patricia brought out a square navy blue box. In it was the triangular gold medal Henry had received from the American Institute of Architects thirty five years earlier for "distinguished creative design and execution, where design and hand craftsmanship are inseparable." The heavy gold medal hung from a navy blue ribbon. According to Veda, Henry had said many times he wanted me to have it. Bill in his grief could part with nothing.

• • •

On the final trip to Memphis, when we returned to transport Henry's tapestry back to the villa, I drove down White Station Road, which had been widened into four lanes for cars. We went up and down the road looking for my old house. Finally, we stopped and on foot realized that the old house and its tiny knolls that sheltered a place of childhood fantasy had been replaced by a commercial store in a short strip of offices. The store had retained, however, the number 717. Further on I found with satisfaction that the Memphis Athletic Club, which had obliterated a place of mystery, had yielded to change. Torn down, a small office park now was located on the site. The traces of my little plantation lay deep within the earth, lost to all except in the memories of worn fields, a haunted house, shiny metal and sweet blackberries, the energy of its Halflife dissipated into a random spray of atoms.

CODA

Many years have passed since I wrote these notes for Halflife. The second half of life has dwindled. Pondering the randomness of recollection, I wonder why certain memories remained and others vanished. Were some lodged in cellular complexes, bound up in a chemical coding, retained in the brain, and others not? The weight of memory calls up the image of a balance. Has there been more pain than happiness, more loss than gain? How does a person measure? Where is the fulcrum? I still grieve the lost ones, family, friends, and lovers. Losing them devoured my innocence as a young man. Resentment and anger from those losses lived within me, affecting my life every day. Does memory expiate pain?

I am the residue of those who have loved me and their gifts are what I have learned about loving. I am still learning how to nurture. I pass on what little I know, distilled into nectar saved in a small brass ampoule. The places are strings of a warp tied in front and back, held in tension by the ratcheting of a cogged wheel on the back beam. The stories lay at right angles, a weft, and the filler for fabric and tapestry, all held whole by tension. Those who loved us and whom we loved emerge in the tissue of fabric, united in warp and weft, color and texture.

Time has marked the body, notching memories of Halflife into it. Only lately am I aware of my heart as a separate organ in my body—not pulse or sound of heart beat but the object itself. Complaining about its own Halflife, it throbs one day early in the fall, hurting as big arteries around it lurch into spasm, acting like nothing more than a muscle in pain. Also, a self consciousness of the skin appears. I had read somewhere that the skin becomes thin with age, but the fact meant little to me. Eventually I could see that scratches and cuts healed more slowly than I remember, that surfaces of the face were more susceptible to abrasion, and the skin became more vulnerable as it grew thinner. The thinness paralleled a tendency to dryness, the fluids drawing up, the eyes less wet with tears, less juice perhaps for the organs within. The Dalai Lama once described the drying of the body as a point of death's journey. Hydration has its limits, so the thinning of skin and the desiccation of the body play their role in Halflife. Skin, thinning, looks like a tent hung over the muscles, bones, arteries, veins, and organs within. No camouflage material, this skin is papery. A few dark spots are scattered as well as small dots without pigment, all presaging the blotchy coloring of old age. What is the Halflife of skin?

Patricia and I eventually moved to live in the mountains where the stories of Halflife began. Santa Fe was utterly different, a destination of international tourism. The rural villages had lost all sense of isolation. The fields filled with houses not crops. But the sky had not changed. Often I wake early at our old adobe house on the edge of town and sit outside by the front door. A breeze that comes over the mountains plays with the rising sun on my face, arms, chest. I had forgotten the quiet of the early morning. No human voices are present, but instead the sounds of a bone rattling in the mouth of a black and white dog, crickets, piñon jays, and other birds are heard. I had forgotten the vista south from the foothills of the Sangre de Christo across a broad plane to the Ortiz and Sandia mountains to the south, a deep vista of sixty miles still showing little visible human presence. I had forgotten the wave inside me, singing, curling with frothy edges, a Hokusai wave contained in a vessel it will soon break. I had forgotten a silent unspeakable force within.

A nameless dog comes up to greet me. He places his head on my arm. Panting, he is delighted with the company of a stranger. He licks my feet and moves off into the shade. The breeze vanishes, and sun becomes very hot. The dog returns, licks my hands, and nuzzles my arm. He wears a blue collar without tags, and has a stub for a tail. The day passes, a breeze returns, cools me, and pours over the dog. A breeze is as much sound as it is the convection of heat and cold. It is an unseen animator, the dog its friend.

Finally, I unpacked the stored tools I had used to make sculpture, the paint brushes, the files, and rasps, a glue pot, and bottles of dark liquids whose labels had faded long ago. As I put the Swiss carving chisels into the canvas apron that housed them, I thought I heard a small voice. I looked down at the number eight chisel as a light glinted off its polished surface. I brought the chisel with its razor sharpness closer to my face. The voice again, faint, emerging from somewhere between the ferrule and the shank, sang out: "We tools want a place for ourselves after the work. We need a shelter, a place of refuge after the work." I was startled and set down the chisel, lined it up with all the other chisels and saw light gleaming in an arc, like the crescent of a moon.

Inanimate objects had spoken to me before, and I knew to heed these voices. The tool's voice was plaintive, even sad, so I took to heart the request and began contemplating a dwelling for my tools. A new place began to emerge, a studio for living with a water wheel, a pond, a hearth and a shelter, so tools had their own home. I began, once again, to make a place of refuge.